I Love You, Daddy

A DDLG and ABDL romantic love story of a tortured woman who finds peace with the love only a Daddy Dom can provide

By Tina Moore

Table of Contents

Chapter 1

"I can save you," he had lovingly said. His blue eyes, and toothy smile begging to be needed, as desperate to be loved as she was. Nadia remembered how she had slowly pulled his blue blazer off and unbuttoned his crisp white shirt revealing his chiseled chest — running her fingers over the curves of his pecks, a shiver running down her spine, giving her arms goosebumps.

"No, you can't," she replied in a whisper, her green eyes wishing that he didn't look at her like she was faultless when all she knew to be true was that she was nothing and worthless.

"Isn't that what you want? I know that if you give me a chance, we would be great together. You don't really think that I'm like those other guys do you?" He had persisted. Nadia had reached up and pushed him away at that point, needing distance as he crept dangerously close to the place she kept her pain.

"Don't. Please, I can't," she said, looking at him, wishing she could trust him but not knowing how.

"So that's it? It's over?" He had angrily asked wanting more of her than she was ready to give him, buttoning his shirt back up. Nadia looked at him through tear glazed eyes wishing that she could be the person he thought she was.

"Call it what you want, I'm not who you think I am," Nadia said, pushing past him and crying as she left the changing room of her workplace.

Nadia had seen him several times after that encounter, each time he tried to get too close to her, she would push him away. Unable to tell him what she truly desired, unable to tell him how she knew she liked what she liked. Always running away from him and anyone else who dared get too close to her. Like a damaged pound pup who would cower in the corner of the cage until being scared didn't work anymore. Baring her teeth and letting out an angry snarl before bolting from the confined space she found herself in, Nadia was always on high alert.

Nadia looked at her reflection in the public bathroom mirror at the department store where she worked. Working for a luxury brand in the city had it's perks, sharing a bathroom with the public was not one of them. As she read the back door advertising for what seemed like the hundredth time, she shook her head knowing that somehow this life was not the one she would always have to live.

A storm which had been raging for days had brought the city to a standstill, and the floors were wet and slippery as Nadia slowly made her way out of the store and towards the front door. She was flexing off work early to miss the swarm of people she knew would be all fighting for a seat on the limited buses which waited just outside the store. True to her prediction, the buses lined up as the bells from the cathedral echoed over the city square, signaling the 5 o'clock finish. As people poured from the buildings which blocked the sky, she looked out from the glass elevator and saw the crowds below. People pushing, cutting in front of each other and grumbling at the long wait to get home.

I guess I'll just walk, she thought to herself as the elevator chimed and the push of the people from the back moved her forward. She pulled her waterproof trench coat tightly around her waist and pulled the hood over her head as she dipped her head and walked through the crowds. She had to get to the over side of the square to take the short cut home. Even without the rain, a walk home would take an hour, and she knew that her shoes would be soaked through by the time she made her way to the other side of the square. She didn't dare think about how ruined they'd be by the time she got home.

"Watch it," came an angry voice to which she ignored, hoping that it wasn't directed at her.

She didn't have the care to turn around and have it out with him, and so decided just to keep walking, hoping to get far away from the angry lines of cold and wet people. Nadia pushed her way through, sighing with relief when she made it to the clearing on the other side and stopped to turn and look at the mass of bodies behind her. Breathing deeply, Nadia decided to take her shoes off and place them in a bag within her work handbag, hoping to preserve them as best she could. Turning back to continue her walk home, she numbed her mind as she walked. She wasn't interested in being in this place anymore; she only wanted to get home. The home where her stuffies waited for her, where she could watch the shows her soul craved and eat snacks that made no sense in the world she was so quickly trying to escape.

I wonder if people look at me and see it, see what I truly desire, she thought, turning a corner and continuing to walk. The rain had chilled her bones to the core, and she shivered as she walked. Her hair falling flat against her head, she took out a hair tie to make a top bun hoping to look slightly more presentable.

I must look so disheveled right now, Nadia almost said out loud, finding herself smirking as she walked around the various puddles on the street and crossing the road, that's when she saw him. Standing against a lamppost, vaping into the rain, his hair slicked back as he ran his fingers through it, seemingly unaware of the storm which thundered around him. Nadia looked at him, standing there, watching as the world turned and wondered how peaceful it must be to remain so calm amid a city in chaos. As if reading her mind, he turned to look at her, smiling as though he had known her for years. Nadia looked away, not wanting to talk to anybody, let alone a strange man but as she slowly looked back at him, she saw that his gaze had not shifted. Nadia smiled back, hoping that a simple smile would satisfy his need for her attention and when he tilted his head at her slowly, she turned the corner and tried to hide the smile which she found to be growing on her face.

"Miss?" Nadia heard him calling after her.

Great, just what I was hoping to avoid, Nadia thought as she turned around.

"You dropped this," he said, holding out her scarf. It was as though the world had stopped turning, and she only saw him. His raven black hair, and blue eyes, his defined jawline, and energy she knew she would be drunk on if she stayed too long.

"Oh, thanks," she replied, reaching out to take the scarf which she tied back onto her bag. Nadia could tell he wanted to talk some more, his twitching lips gave him away, but as she raised an eyebrow, she liked how he decided to let go of whatever he had found so pressing.

"Bye," Nadia said, trying to give him a hint and watched as he took a step back and smiled his knowing smile again before disappearing out of sight.

Weird, she thought, turning around as well and continued the three blocks until she was home.

Nadia opened her door and dropped everything in the doorway as she walked into the bathroom, turned on the shower and crept the hot water up slowly as she warmed her body with each turn on the tap. She had wished she could stop thinking about the guy with her scarf, how his hand been soft and his nails manicured, his face clean-shaven and his business suit soaked through and clinging to his solid form. Leaving the shower, she wrapped her body in her fluffy pink towel, surprising herself as she thought how he would feel holding her as she walked into her bedroom, knowing that she would have to diaper herself for another evening.

Going to her drawer, she took out the pink onesie with the frills on the sleeve, took her blankie and bunny and crawled to the sofa before she put on the movie. Sighing, Nadia fell into her little space as she fell asleep, curled up in a cocoon of blankie and big soft pillows, happy to finally escape the day.

Nadia woke up with a fright, having to remind herself where she was as the house was in complete darkness. She reached for the phone she had left it on the side table next to her sofa and checked the time. It was past midnight as the screen blinded her with its bright background, and as she remembered that she had left her wet clothes on the tiled entrance, she sighed and got up. She walked over to the mess she had left behind, taking her clothes to the laundry and putting them in the washing machine before going to the kitchen and putting some frozen snacks in the oven. She crawled back over to her nest on the sofa and snuggled in as she looked through her handbag and took out her shoes and it was then that she saw the note the man had slipped into her bag when he had handed the scarf back. It was his business card.

Typical, she thought to herself, rolling her eyes as she turned the card over to see something a little more personal.

I know it's a bit of a cliché, but if you'd like to

get to know me, I'll be having coffee at 9:30 Saturday morning at café 86, Jason, the back of the card read.

Well, that is awfully bold of him, Nadia thought trying not to smirk and put the card down. She was hungry, and although his note was intriguing, her dino nuggies really did take priority.

Nadia spent the rest of the week thinking about Saturday, if she would go or if she would just sit at another table and watch him.

He might have given that card out to heaps of girls; Nadia thought as she ate her lunch in the back room at work Friday afternoon. She looked at the expensive bags and munched on her salad as she looked at the colors of the bags she knew she would never be able to afford. Nadia flipped a coin and chose heads to go and tails to stay at home, watching as the coin flipped in the air, she caught it and placed it on the back of her hand. Heads.

Guess I'm having coffee with Jason, she

thought to herself, finished the last mouthful of salad and smiled, excited to be meeting him in less than 24 hours.

Nadia had arrived at the café 15 minutes early and looked out for him.

This might be the dumbest thing you have ever done; she thought as she waited for him and shook her head and laughed in disbelief as he sat down and smiled back at her when he saw Nadia sitting in the café.

"I'm so glad you came!" He said taking the paper napkin and flamboyantly placed it over his lap before looking at her expectantly.

"I'm Jason," he said, extending his hand and offering it to her. Nadia rolled her eyes, and with playful reluctance shook his hand.

"I'm Nadia," she said, as the waitress come to the table. Nadia ordered a peppermint mocha with extra sprinkles, and as she watched the woman walk away, all she wished was that the waitress would come back with her order so she could hide behind the cup.

"So, do you do that a lot?" Nadia asked, wanting to fill the silence that had begun to fall between them.

"Actually, no. But when I saw you a few days ago, I thought, I need to talk to this woman," Jason said as his coffee arrived in front of him. Nadia looked at him, he was perfect, and she couldn't believe that she was sitting with him in this place.

"Well, I hope you aren't a serial killer or something. That would really piss me off because there's this handbag that I'm saving really hard to buy. So, let me have the success of buying it before you know, you chop me up," Nadia half-joked, clutching the warm cup of drink that the busty waitress had only just placed in front of her.

"I'm not a serial killer, but I like your drive. Tell me about the handbag," Jason said, making her laugh.

"You don't want to hear about that," she said, shaking her head and taking a sip of the warm sweet liquid.

"Yes, I do actually," Jason said gently, making Nadia laugh and look at him suspiciously.

"Ok, here it is," she said, opening her phone and showing him the photo of her dream bag. Jason spent a lot of time looking at the photo, making Nadia wonder what he was thinking. When he finally looked up, he looked at her with a seriousness she had seen in most of the men she had dated, almost making her disappointed that he resembled them.

"So, what's your budget like, because if you want that bag, you could have it very easily," Jason said, finishing his coffee in one gulp.

"Um, my budget?" Nadia asked. She had been with financial doms before, but they had always let her down so swinging to the opposite extreme, she lived somewhat paycheck to paycheck.

"Yeah. You don't have one, do you?" Jason asked knowingly. Nadia just shrugged her shoulders and looked out the window.

"Hey, I'm not chipping you. I want to help you," Jason said softly, reaching out to touch her hand.

"Why?" She questioned angrily feeling judged and vulnerable and pulling her hand away.

"Because I'm drawn to you, Nadia. I can't explain it; I just want to be around you and help you have the best life you can," Jason said. She grimaced at him, unable to process what was being said to me.

"Then ask me out on a real date," she asked, waiting for him expectantly, but he just shook his head.

"No. You ask me. Because I've already chosen you, so, if you want me, you'll have to choose me too. Maybe we should," he began to say, but all she heard was the noise in her mind. The piercing scream from all the places she kept locked away and out of reach. Her mind always went there. More than she wished it would. It was exhausting, and yet it was in the exhaustion she had learned to feel peace. Maybe it wasn't even peace she was feeling; maybe it was just her body being too fractured to continue, and in the silence and surrender she could at least be still.

"Dude, I met you like five minutes ago, chill," Nadia said gesturing dramatically, coming back into the room and distancing herself from him. Jason just smirked and nodded before looking out the window to the people on the street.

Chapter 2

"The aquarium? That's where you want to go?" Jason asked, surprised that Nadia had called him and was deep in, organizing a date, mode late Thursday afternoon of the following week.

"Yep. Do you want to come or not?" She asked, keeping her guard up. She had been with guys like him before. The beautiful ones, the ones who knew how desirable they were and was cautious not to make the same mistake with him she had made with other men.

"Alright then, I'll pick you up at 9? Maybe after we could get brunch?" Jason suggested. Nadia just looked from side to side in her living room, unsure if this was a good idea or not.

"I'm good; I'll meet you out the front of the aquarium at 9 o'clock on Saturday. Ok bye," she said before quickly hanging up. She threw her phone onto the sofa and brought her knees to her chest, hyperventilating and staring into space. Happy she was taking a chance on him, but nervous as hell. Deciding she should go for a run, Nadia got up and walked to her cupboard and looked at her little things, wondering how long she would entertain the idea of Jason before sharing with him one of the essential parts of her life. She pushed the thought from her mind and pulled on her activewear, tieing her hair in a messy ponytail and tearing the skin from her cuticle as she walked out the door enjoying the pain and watching as blood pooled along her nailbed. Tensing her calves as the elevator levels flashed on the display screen, Nadia exhaled deeply as two people got into the lift on the 3rd floor. She was happy she had her earphones in her ears so they wouldn't talk to her but returned their smile before looking up at the ceiling.

We need to stop teaching people these bullshit cultural gestures, that's one more smile I'm never getting back, Nadia bitterly thought to herself as she exited the lift and ran from the building not wanting to have to share the space with the friendly strangers for another moment.

She ran like a Brumby from a paddock, letting the cold night air choke her throat as she reminded herself that life was temporary, nothing more or less than moments in time. She hid behind the dark shades that filled the night's sky as she fought back, her tears feeling herself try to run away from the gentlest of monsters who had reached in and ripped the innocence from her soul. The warmth of where his hands had been on her body; still present and never fading. The face that Nadia saw, haunting her as she closed her eyes to fall asleep at night alone and lonely despite her bed almost always being full. The smile Nadia wished she could see again but wanting more than anything she could forget. She frowned as she panted, annoyed that she didn't have a better strategy to numb her pain. She felt like she had never stopped running. It tired her body, but it was her mind she was so desperately trying to silence. It helped her stop thinking when she gasped for air just trying to stay conscious. She tried to say his name as she ran, but the word refused to escape her lips. She could only refer to her nightmare as *him*. So she ran, feeling her body fueled by pain and rage and the memory of a thousand lives she had tried to live since then. And yet, in a moment of remembrance, she was back there. With his body behind her's, whispering in her ear how her body was made for fucking as he slowly felt her under her baby pink pajama shorts.

Goosebumps made her shiver as he kissed the bare tanned skin her white racerback singlet exposed. It had all been so exciting until it wasn't. She remembered how she had liked the noticeable change in the air when she had first seen him and how that mighty wind had stayed for several days after. From a gentle breeze, it grew into a fierce and frightening wind. From swaying trees so peaceful and calm to a violent shaking, daring the branches to bend to breaking point. From trees that were full but filled with nothing but death, to being stripped bare yet only life was left on their branches. The wind was him. Destroying anything that stopped him from what his desires were with relentless ambition, refusing to surrender. Everything about him reflected in one of natures most catastrophically dangerous and uniquely beautiful elements. It didn't surprise Nadia that she had given into him.

How do you refuse a force that exposes your vulnerabilities yet keeps you completely safe from harm? Nadia thought as she doubled over and pulled air from the bottom of her lungs, dry reaching as she remembered how he whispered, *shh Daddy's got you baby girl* when she whimpered and tried to pull away from him.

Was I ever even safe, though, like, this shit doesn't feel very fucking safe, it's ruined my whole fucking life. Was it all just a play to get what he wanted? Did he know that I wouldn't put up a fight? Did he see how my eyes begged to be held? Why do they have the same look in them after all this time? She questioned angrily, knowing that answers to her questions would never be answered. Nadia stood back up and tasted the blood from her dry mouth as she tried to stop the dizziness taking over her body.

He never gave a shit about you; you get that right? You were just something to do, something to pass the time. And you did all that, everything he asked, for what? A fucking hug? Cause Mommy and Daddy fought? Cause no one ever tucked you in at night? Cause there was no one there when you cried when you scraped your knee? Shit. Grow up, bitch. Do you know how much easier life would have been if you just like, weren't so fucking needy? Weren't such a slut, just so fucking easy? Nadia felt her heart whine as she dipped her head and raced up a hill. With him, Nadia saw a reality she had only ever seen in her wildest dreams.

Maybe Jason won't be like, him? Perhaps I was just too young when he showed me all this. Maybe Jason won't ask for so much? Maybe it won't be as bad, maybe he isn't even into this, and I'm just wasting my time, Nadia almost said out loud as she broke back into a military paced run.

It would have been so much easier if it was anyone but him. Why can't I shake this when it's everything but right? Why does it have such a hold over me? Why do I still feel his touch when it was years ago? Why does my body still shiver with anticipation when I think of his hand on my tummy, holding me in place? Was I always going to like this, always into this? Or do I only like it because he showed it to me? Nadia thought, wishing she hadn't seen him every day for the next three and a half years.

She tortured herself as she regretted not being able to prove she was the woman society had raised her to be. She was stuck with the memory, the sadness, the wetness, and the shame. Replaying on constant repeat all the acts she had performed that proved she just wasn't the same as the other girls she had grown up with. It would have been nice to be someone like them. But that just wasn't her. The invisible lines Nadia had circled around herself to stay confined, controlled, socially accepted, and tamed had been ripped open and left bare by him. And as Nadia felt the power he still had over her flooding her senses, she knew all too well, what that sweet, wicked smile of Jason's meant.

"Whatever, fuck it. Never again, straight up, never again will I let someone treat me like that. And if that means I never have a Daddy again and only have some quick turn over, pretend relationship, then so fucking be it," Nadia said out loud as she walked into her apartment building deciding that it was better to be alone than ever feel the need of wanting someone ever again.

"I was starting to think you stood me up," Jason joked as Nadia walked quickly to meet him.

"Yeah sorry, something came up," she said, putting her hands in her pockets.

"What?" Jason asked, making Nadia bite her bottom lip.

"I said something came up," she repeated, unsure why he was smiling.

"Yeah I know, what came up?" He asked, causing Nadia to pulled an annoyed face.

"What are you? A detective?" She replied defensively, only causing Jason to laugh.

"No, I just want to get to know you, you look good," he replied, walking with Nadia as she began to enter the aquarium.

"I get that a lot, try something else," Nadia said, instantly irritated by his eagerness.

"Well, how about this? You are beautiful when you're angry," Jason teased, his face going from smoulderingly alluring to stupid puppy dog in an instant making Nadia stop and turn to look at him.

This is a complete waste of my time, Nadia thought as she looked him dead in the eye.

"Look. This isn't going to happen. Don't follow me. Sorry, take care," she replied, leaving him standing next to a big fish hanging from the ceiling in the foyer. Walking out, Nadia breathed in surrender to her feelings as she began to walk home, happy that Jason hadn't bothered to follow her.

I think I stunned him; she thought as she blocked his number. Walking through the city, Nadia tried to feel anything but the breaking of her heart.

Maybe he would have been nice; perhaps he would have been everything I want, she thought as she haled a taxi. Rolling her eyes, she exhaled and shook her head as she looked up the roof of the smoke-smelling cab. She told the driver her address and slumped down in the backseat, tears escaping her eyes, wishing she could outrun herself. She didn't even really know what she was crying for; all she knew was that it hurt. In the center of her chest like someone had punched and winded her, it hurt. The words past lovers had shared as their parting message, sticking to her like glue. That she was cold, detached, unapproachable, so beautiful but angry, Nadia loved that one the most.

Yeah, I'm fucking angry you dumb fucks, she thought to herself.

How can I not be? You don't fucking know what it's like as much as you all like to pretend you do, she added remembering how everyone had been so devoted to her recovery until they realized that she would never be the girl they wished she was, as the taxi stopped and pulled up outside her door.

Chapter 3

Nadia stayed in bed for the rest of the day, deep in her little space as she tried to numb her pain.

This shit is getting old, she thought, angry that she hadn't figured out how to shake the heavy blackness that lay like a blanket over her.

All I want is a Daddy who will love me. I didn't think that was so hard to ask for, she thought, stripping out of her onesie and diaper and going to the shower.

Running the hot water over her body, she placed both hands on the shower wall, dipped her head, and cried as the water scorched her skinny frame. She yelled, knowing that once again, no one would be able to hear her.

Getting out, she walked naked through the living room and into the kitchen, took an apple slice from her unicorn container and then went back to her room, getting dressed in adult pajamas just as a knock came from the door. Hesitantly, she walked to it, putting the chain in the lock and opening it slowly.

"Hey, I've just moved in next door, and I heard yelling or something coming from here, are you ok?" A man softly said as he dipped his head down to try and meet Nadia's gaze. She was busy looking at his shoes.

Crocodile leather boots, Nadia thought, impressed with his choice and slowly lifting her head. Taking in the man's black wrangler jeans and his green button-down shirt, his eyes kind and gentle and his hair thick and wavey.

"Oh yeah, sorry, I hadn't realized that anyone had moved in yet," Nadia said, feeling embarrassed standing in front of him in her pajamas. He continued to stare at her until Nadia become uncomfortable and shifted her gaze from left to right.

"What do you want?" She softly asked, wanting him to stop looking at her.

"Nothing, my name is Dan, if you need anything, you can always come and ask. Have a good night," Dan said, turning to go back into his apartment.

"Dan, I'm Nadia," she quickly said as he reached his door. Turning around, Dan looked at her plainly, giving her a half-smile and tipping his head slightly before opening his door and shutting it behind him.

Shit, Nadia thought, closing her door and biting her bottom lip.

Well, he heard you, she amusingly said to herself as she started to tidy up her toys.

Over the next three weeks, Nadia had seen Dan four times in the lift, at the local supermarket and had even run into him at her work. He had been looking for a new business suit, and she had directed him to the most expensive suits in the store.

"I know what you are doing," Dan said, smiling in the mirror as he tried on the jacket.

Nadia just rolled her eye dramatically.

"Come on, help a girl out," She just laughed back, happy when Dan passed her his card.

"Well, better go ring these up then," he said, passing her the jacket, matching trousers and shirt and walking back into the changing room with only his own jeans on, his bare chest catching more eyes than just Nadia's.

Oh my god, he is beautiful, she thought walking away to the cash register and waiting for him to come back.

"Hey, Nadia, look I know you're going to want to say no, but," he said pausing to look at her. He saw how she was already thinking of a way to get out of what he was about to say, so he just smiled and shook his head.

"No, what, tell me," she said, seeing how he gave up on her but not wanting him to.

"There's an art gallery opening in town tomorrow night. I want to go, but these things can be so, pretentious, it's nice to have someone there to, you know, fight off the snobby art people. They also make for excellent entertainment and people watching," Dan said, happy to see the smile spread across Nadia's lips.

"You sold it just right, what time?" She asked, surprising herself at how open and excited she was to be spending the evening with him. Dan gestured for the piece of paper behind the counter and took out a pen from his pocket before writing down the address and a time.

"I'll meet you there, see you later," he said, taking the suit bag Nadia bought around to the front of the counter, smiling despite herself and desperate to see him again.

She raced home as fast as she could and took her time searching through the photos of the art gallery looking at the type of dresses other women wore to events like this. Deciding to go with a pink, backless cocktail dress with silver strappy heels, Nadia laid the outfit on her sofa and went to bed feeling the anticipation of having all of Dan's attention.

"Wow, look at you," he said as he saw her walk up to the door of the quaint gallery. She had to stop herself from blushing at his compliment and saw that he was wearing the pants to the suit he had bought the day earlier.

"Nice pants, someone dressed you well," Nadia replied, stopping to kiss him on the cheek before she could stop herself.

Fuck, I hope that was ok, she thought to herself in a panic and slowly stepped back to look at Dan.

"Soft lips," was all he said as he held out his hand to her and walked her inside.

"So, are we pretending to be a loving power couple?" Nadia teased as Dan took two glasses of champagne from the tray that passed them and offered her a glass. Accepting, they made a silent toast before Dan eyed her suspiciously as he took a sip.

"If you'd like. But I was thinking of something a little more. Baby," Dan said, whispering the word baby in Nadia's ear and almost making her choke. She looked up at him with fear in her eyes, clearly not hiding as well as she had thought she had. Dan just held her gaze, blocking her way when she tried to leave.

"Don't run away. There's nowhere to go. You'll have to talk to me like a big girl for a moment," he said, watching how Nadia tried to find a way to escape.

"What do you want? A fucking medal for figuring it out? It's hardly that exciting," she aggressively said, downing her drink and placing the glass on the next tray which passed. Dan just smirked and slowly walked out of the gallery, causing Nadia to stand alone in the room full of strangers before chasing after him.

"Wait," she said, once they were alone on the street. Dan stopped and turned around, kindness pouring from his eyes.

"How did you know?" She curiously asked, coming to stand next to him before grabbing his hand and leading him into the nearest bar she could find. Dan let her lead, finding it endearing that she was trying so hard to face something she was clearly uncomfortable enjoying.

"Are you sure you want to know?" Dan asked, sitting down at a dirty table, making him laugh at how badly they stood out compared to the other patrons who sat around, looking at the way Nadia was dressed. Nadia nodded her head and waited patiently for Dan to order two beers before coming back to sit next to her. Placing the drinks down on the table, he ran his fingers through his hair and thought for a moment before speaking.

"It's the way you feel. I can just tell. You're hurting, badly, and I think you keep that little space right behind the wall you use to block out the world because it all just feels so overwhelming and simply too, everything," Dan said, instantly annoying Nadia who hated how easily he had read her.

"Whatever," she said, rolling her eyes and wishing that she could let herself go and relax for once.

"See?" Dan teased, making Nadia roll her

eyes as she drank the beer in silence.

"You want to go home?" Dan asked, seeing that Nadia was feeling restless. She just nodded, not knowing how to place herself or what headspace to be in, her world felt as though it was spinning, and she couldn't seem to find a feeling to hold onto.

"It's alright Nadia, I'm not going to hurt you, you can trust me," Dan said, opening a taxi door and waiting for her to get in first. She just grimaced at his words and held her breath as she gave him a chance, hoping with all she had that he would be true to his word.

"Do you want to come inside for a drink?" He asked as the city lights rushed past them. Nadia just shrugged her shoulders. She had not been this close to a guy in years. Usually, she would have been long gone by now, and it frightened her to be so physically close to someone.

"I don't know," she said, hoping that he would leave due to her indecisiveness, but Dan just gently smiled at her, slowly reached for her hand and gazed at her in the most unthreatening of ways.

"How about, I just leave my door open and if you want to come in, you can and then if you want to leave, of course, you can do that too," he suggested, making Nadia nod her head as the taxi pulled up outside their apartment building. Dan paid the man and rushed over to Nadia's side as she entered the building. As they reached the elevator, Nadia silently reached for Dan's hand and held it loosely as the lights flicked in ascending order until they stopped on level 10.

"Well, I'll see you if I see you," he said, letting her hand go lovingly before opening his door and walking inside, leaving it open for Nadia who looked in. From what she could see, he had polished concrete floors, white walls with sizeable colorful artwork hanging prominently, and a modern kitchen. Nadia found herself wondering what the rest of his place looked like as she moved towards his doorway and rested against the wall.

"Woah, nice," she involuntarily said as she

looked into the living room and saw the generous leather couches and soft rug in the middle of the floor.

"Your ceilings look higher than mine," she added with a frown. Dan just laughed as he watched her from the kitchen. He had made hot chocolate for both of them and placed the cup on the kitchen counter for Nadia.

"It's just the placing of the furniture. Here, would you like some marshmallows?" Dan said, holding the cup up to Nadia who shifted nervously in the doorway, backing away slowly.

"No, I didn't see you make it, I have no idea what's in there," Nadia said, finding herself feel more confident. Dan just tilted his head, the thought of hurting Nadia had never crossed his mind, but finding out that it had clearly crossed hers, he thought for a moment, watching as her eyes remained unwavering in her decision.

It must be so stressful being a woman and having to be on the highest of guards all the time; he thought as he nodded his head and tipped it down the sink.

"Well, how about you watch me make this one then?" He suggested, seeing Nadia walk into the living room and stopping by the couches. She just nodded her head, and meekly smiled at him as she rested her head on her hands and watched.

"First I'll warm the milk, I just used normal full cream, but I have almond if you prefer," Dan said, opening the fridge.

"Almond, cows milk freaks me out, like just no," Nadia said, making Dan laugh.

"I feel like I should have just known," he said, taking out a mug.

"Now I'm going to heat it," he continued, stopping when Nadia shook her head.

"You have to put the chocolate in next," Nadia corrected as Dan looked at her in confusion.

"Trust me," she added, watching how he soften and followed her instructions.

"Now you heat it," she said when she was satisfied with the level of chocolate Dan had scooped into the mug.

"You'll give yourself diabetes if this is how you take your hot chocolate," he laughed as he waited for the microwave to count down to zero and beep. Taking it out, he stirred it before taking out two marshmallows only to have Nadia have a mild panic attack and race over to the kitchen where he was standing and take the two pink ones from his hands.

"They don't taste nice, I only like the white ones," she said, finding two white ones for the drink and two for her trip back to the couch. Dan laughed, bringing their drinks over to where she stood and sat down on the couch. Dan looked at her, assuming that she would sit but seeing that she remained standing, he stood up again.

"I have never experienced anyone quite like you Nadia," he laughed, sipping his drink.

"White marshmallows are not a game. Honestly, I don't know why they bother making any other flavor," Nadia laughed, feeling more relaxed and deciding to sit, sitting cross-legged on the couch facing Dan who joined her.

"Is this the part where we make small talk?" Nadia said in a voice that made Dan smile.

"I don't care about small talk, and I don't care about talking at all if you don't want to. But if you do want to fill the silence, why don't you ask me some questions," Dan said, leaning into the couch. Nadia just looked at him and wondered how she had been so lucky to have his attention. She knew she wasn't easy to get along with, everyone had always told her how awful she was, but he didn't seem to mind her defenses. He didn't take it personally as everyone else had. They had wanted her trust, her affection, her obedience with only a command to be given, without having earned it, without asking her if she had even wanted them.

Nadia let the silence build between the two of them long after their drinks were finished before speaking again.

"Tell me about this piece. You sold me on a night full of art gazing, and all that I got was a glass of average champagne," Nadia playfully said as she got up and walked to the artwork which hung in the corridor. Dan stayed sitting on the couch, stretched his arms out, and rested his head back.

"It's a piece I did in high school. It feels about 500 years ago now, but we had to do self-portraits. Everyone did their face, but I even in the whirlwind of my 17-year-old self, I knew that my face was not who I was, so I tried to paint my soul. I failed senior art because of it, but it didn't bother me because I knew I hadn't really failed, I had just failed the system that I was being assessed in. It is one of my proudest accomplishments," Dan said, opening his eyes again to see Nadia standing in front of him.

"That's a lot deeper than I thought you'd be," she said, sitting down next to him. He tried to hide the excitement in his eyes at how close she was, but his toothy smile gave him away, causing Nadia to roll her eyes.

"I guess I can surprise you too li," he said, stopping himself from calling her little one. She seemed to be aware of the words he wanted to speak because she just smiled to the side and looked down before looking back up at him.

"You can you know," she said softly, hoping she had read him right.

"What," he said, matching her softness.

"Call me little one," Nadia hesitantly said, biting her bottom lip nervously. Dan just smiled and opened his arms to her and watched as she slowly came closer until her body pressed against his in a loving embrace.

"You are everything you think you're not darling," he said, feeling Nadia's body relaxing slowly in his arms. She closed her eyes to try and stop the tears from escaping her eyes as Dan thumbed them away.

"You're alright, nothing bad will happen to you when you're with me. I'm not going to hurt you," he gently said, rocking her slightly as she cried.

Chapter 4

"I wasn't expecting to hear from you so soon little one," Dan said down the phone the following day. He and Nadia had said goodnight in the early hours of the morning and had only been apart for a few hours when his phone had lit up.

"Yeah, I hope you don't think I'm too clingy or whatever?" Nadia said, concerned that he didn't want to talk to her so soon.

"Not at all, what are you up too?" He asked, hearing Nadia sigh down the phone as she got comfortable.

"I've been thinking about what you said last night, how you suggested that we see if this is something that could work for both of us. I'd like to try," she said, holding her breath. It had been hard enough for her to summon the courage to ring him; she really hoped that he wouldn't deny her request.

"I'd love that!" Dan exclaimed, catching Nadia off guard and making her giggle with excitement.

"Cool," she said, unsure of what to say but wanting Dan to know that she was still interested in the conversation.

"Yeah, it is. So, would you like to go somewhere and talk about a few things?" He suggested, walking to the kitchen and taking a pen and notepad from the top drawer.

"Ok, um, do you want to come to mine, I've seen your place, so it's only fair," Nadia said, happy when she heard Dan laugh.

"Yes, and I fully plan to tell you how to make my coffee to return the favor of your instructions from last night," he teased, making Nadia smile and look around her apartment. She had cleaned it in anticipation for his arrival.

"When are you free?" Dan said, interrupting her train of thought.

"Um, like now?" Nadia laughed, hearing

Dan's door open. She rushed to the door, opening it up to see him standing in his pajama's still on the phone.

"I'm not ready yet," he laughed. Nadia liked how playful he was and tilted her head as she looked at his pajama's. His grey sweat pants and tight white t-shirt made his chest muscles look even bigger than they were.

"Wait there," Nadia said before running back into her apartment, leaving the door open and quickly changing into her pajama's. She wore short red shorts and a grey racerback singlet, the thin straps of her red bra showing against the newly toned muscles of her back. Coming back to where Dan was waiting patiently, he laughed as he saw her.

"Cute," he said, looking at her with a gleam in his eye.

"We can have a pajama party," Nadia said, smiling as she hung up the phone and waved for Dan to come over.

"Alright alright," Dan said, looking around

her place. She had designed her house with a rustic country flare, a cowhide rug on the living room floor and a large white fabric sofa with European pillows making it look like the white marshmallows of her hot chocolate from the previous night. A fluffy pink throw hung over the side of the sofa, and her kitchen looked like something from a magazine. The modern country fixtures made her place look warm and homely, and as Dan stood in front of the wall covered in black and white photos in pinewood frames, he saw the moments of her life.

"This is lovely," he said, turning back around to face her.

"Thanks," she replied, standing in the kitchen by the coffee machine.

"How'd you like it?" Nadia asked, looking at Dan expectantly. He just chuckled as he walked over and stood next to her.

"Well, first off, I like the milk to go in first," he said, shaking his head when Nadia tried to speak.

"No no, I told you I would show you how I like it," Dan said playfully.

"But that's backward," Nadia replied, rolling her eyes. Dan just raised an eyebrow and waited for her to follow his instructions. As she did, he came around the front of the counter and watched her from the barstool.

"Next, I like the chocolate sprinkles," he said, trying to keep a straight face.

"You are legit just making this up as you go along now," Nadia said, as Dan passed her the vanilla syrup.

"And then two teaspoons of this," he said and went to get her the teaspoon. She stirred in the syrup and looked at him dramatically.

"And now the coffee, just you wait, you've never tasted it so good before," Dan reassured her as she just rolled her eyes and poured the coffee in. Passing it to him, he took a dramatic sip before giving it to her.

"Here, try it," he said, nodding his head. Taking the cup in both her hands, Nadia lifted it to her lips and was surprised by how smooth and creamy the drink was, her eyes popping as she looked at Dan.

"Oh my god, how? I've made vanilla lattes before, and they never taste this good. I better make another one," Nadia said, putting the cup back down.

"Because I've drunk yours," she laughed, going to the cupboard and taking out another cup. Dan laughed in surprise.

"I don't know how I feel about that," he said, shocked that she had finished his drink.

"You are a sneaky one Nadia," he said with a smile as he tucked the information away in the back of his mind.

"What sort of things should we talk about?" Nadia said, bringing over the drink she had just made him and gesturing that they should sit on the sofa. Dan followed as he watched her muscled bare thighs and ass and felt his cock wanting to rip her shorts off and bury himself inside of her.

"How into it are you?" Dan said, sitting

down and placing a pillow on the floor. Nadia just looked at him and blushed.

"Um," she said, unsure of how to answer the question.

"Ok, how about I just say stuff, and you say yes or no?" Dan said, seeing Nadia go shy but nodding her head.

"Alright. This will be like 20 questions. Diapers?" Dan said making Nadia bite her bottom lip and nod her head.

"Do you use them or just like being in them?" He added, sipping his coffee.

"Just being in them, but not all the time," Nadia replied softly. Dan smiled and opened his arms to her as he had done the previous night and watched as she hurried over to his side, clinging to him desperately.

"I'm assuming you like to have a paci, blankie, stuffies, and cute clothes?" Dan said as Nadia nodded her response.

"Cute sippy cups and bowls? Bottle feeding?" Dan continued stopping as Nadia stood up and took his hand, leading him into the spare room she had converted into a nursery. Dan looked around the room and smiled at her knowingly.

"Got it," he said, lifting her and holding her in his arms as she placed her head down on his shoulder.

"See, Daddy?" Nadia said, nervously saying Daddy, hoping that Dan wanted to be hers.

"Daddy sees little one," he lovingly replied as he sat down on the rocking chair and rocked her gently.

"I think we are going to be very happy together, baby girl. You're everything that Daddy has been looking for," Dan said, reaching down to the stuffie on the floor and giving Nadia little kisses with it. She didn't believe that she was everything he had been looking for for a moment, and as he sensed her disbelief, he kissed her forehead.

"Why don't you show Daddy which toys are your favorite?" Dan said, gently putting Nadia down on the floor and watching as she crawled over to the large toy box in the corner of the room. She pulled out one stuffie after another, throwing them on the floor behind her until she found the one she was looking for right at the bottom of the wooden box.

"If it's your favorite, what is it doing at the bottom baby girl?" Dan said, sitting on the floor and opening his arms to Nadia who crawled over to him, sitting in his lap and playing with the purple and blue octopus she had just found.

"She's an octy, Daddy, she lives at the bottom of the ocean," Nadia explained to a nodding Dan.

"Oh, I see now little one. What's octy's name?" Dan said stroking Nadia's hair, surprised how deep and quickly she went into her little space.

"Squidly," she replied confidently, holding it up to Dan's face. He just laughed and watched how Nadia played, wondering how their dynamic had changed.

For the rest of the afternoon, Dan and Nadia played, Dan, being introduced to all the little things Nadia enjoyed and seeing how she beamed up at him whenever he called her a good girl. As the night settled in, he yawned, causing Nadia to look at him curiously.

"Daddy, is it your bedtime?" Nadia giggled as she hid behind a toy and her blankie.

"Daddy doesn't have a bedtime, but I bet you do," he replied, checking his watch.

"We better get you some din-dins and a bath now, or you'll be a little grumpy thing," he said, standing up from the coloring in table and accidentally knocking her block tower down.

"Daddy!" Nadia exclaimed, frantically trying to rebuild her construction. Helping her, Dan knelt and followed her instructions for the next half an hour as they rebuilt the masterpiece.

"Alright, that's enough now sweetie," Dan said, lifting her and holding her firmly as he walked her to the kitchen. Placing her down on the wooden chair at the dining table and looked in the fridge.

"What have we got here, sweetie?" He asked more to himself than to Nadia. She just shrugged her shoulders, suddenly seeming to be unaware what the contents of her fridge. Taking out some vegan burgers, tomato, and lettuce, he went to work cooking up healthy burgers. Coming over to the table as Nadia watched him, he placed down the cut-up burger in front of her and fed her as he ate his own.

"Come on little one, just a few more bites," Dan said as Nadia became fussy and refused to eat.

"No Daddy," she said, shaking her head dramatically from side to side.

"No, Daddy?" Dan questioned, making Nadia giggle before looking at him in the eye.

"Didn't you hear about the little girl who said no, Daddy?" He asked, smiling when Nadia excepted another bite. She just chewed politely as her big eyes looked at him.

"She got a spanking, and it hurt so much that she cried. Do you want to cry tonight, baby girl?" Dan asked, finishing off his meal. He saw how Nadia willingly excepted each mouthful he fed her and smiled.

"Well?" He prompted, Nadia quickly shaking her head no and looking at him fearfully.

"I didn't think so. Alright, little lady, let's get you down, and you can play until bath time," Dan said, taking the plates, and cups into the kitchen and tidying up as Nadia crawled around the living room and played with the train set.

Chapter 5

"Trauma is a funny thing," her therapist said at her next appointment. Nadia didn't even know why she was sitting in the room; it's not like anything could be changed. It happened, it all happened, and pretending that something else happened instead was cute for about five minutes. Nadia wanted to yell at the woman sitting in front of her, ask her what she was meant to do at 2 in the morning when she tried to drink herself to ruin. Scream at her for answers as she sat there, listening to a story that she couldn't understand why was being shared.

Why is she so confusing, how has this story got anything to do with me? Nadia questioned, hoping that her eyes wouldn't give her away, the woman already thought she had an attitude, she didn't want to piss her off any more than she already unknowingly had. The last thing she wanted was to have opened up to her just for her to turn around and leave as well. Nadia looked at the wall and wished she could stand up and smash a hole in it, to say that the woman didn't care about her progress, that she didn't care about her at all.

You're just a paycheck, don't forget that, that's all you mean to her. That's all you've ever been, Nadia said as she looked up at the clock on the wall.

Just another pretender, don't forget that she doesn't give a flying fuck about you. You're only here to sort yourself out; she'd lose no sleep if you never woke again just like the rest of them, Nadia told herself as she smiled at the woman who sat in front of her.

"You're angry, that's understandable," the therapist said writing down something making Nadia wish she could read.

No shit, good observation, better write that down too. Nadia is angry that she got fucked up as a kid, Nadia bitterly said to herself as she sat there plainly, unsure of what answer was appropriate.

Why can't you just take it all away? She thought, looking at the woman with all her experience, success, and wisdom.

If you know so fucking much tell me what to do to fix this, I can't feel like this for much longer. Just tell me what you want, what do I need to do to feel better?! Nadia silently screamed, begging from the deepest parts of her soul, wondering if the woman could hear her desperate cry. Nadia looked up as she saw the woman talking but couldn't hear the words she was saying.

I will do anything. Please fix this, please, she begged, defeated and having to surrender to her pain once again as the door closed behind her and she walked out of the office deciding that she needed to go for a run. Trying to shake the emotions that choked her heart, she walked swiftly up the street and towards her apartment. Her breathing coming in shallow gasps as she saw the fog escaping her mouth as the winter night began to cover the city like a wet blanket.

Nadia let the cold air strip her throat as her feet pounded the pavement. This was her escape, her release, her mental health strategy and the only thing that could stop the thoughts in her head from spinning so wildly that she crashed on her bedroom floor and let one panic attack wash over her after another. Deciding that her demise wasn't an option, she routinely pulled herself together for as long as her day demanded. She had been captain of the track team, and led her team to victory, taking them to the state finals. She had the type of beauty that prompted questioning of a modeling career by relatives at family reunions. She was the perfect daughter, successful, courageous, determined, but no one saw who she truly was. She was the one who screamed her broken heart into her pillow until she tasted blood in her throat every night. The one who people loved to be loved by, with leftover innocence freely given to others until they weren't satisfied anymore and discarded her. Leaving her with nothing but a coldness that seemed to creep down her spine and coil around her throat, her heart being glued together with ice.

The coldness had been apart of her for as long as she could remember. It had settled in after that night, the one she didn't want to remember. The one with the guy who had told her that, *Daddy was there,* only to leave her in the morning. A guy who had been the first to show her what gentleness was, the one who had taken her to the surface after she had been drowning for years. She had thought he would have been there after that, he had said he would, but he had left and in his wake given her a working pattern. One where she chose who had her, and when they left. She had blurred the lines, consenting to the things she didn't want to only to try and find something more painful than what he had done to her so that he wasn't the pinnacle of her pain.

"Hey," Dan said, as Nadia turned the corner and ran into him. It was late and dark, and she wasn't expecting to see anyone out on the street, let alone him. She stood in front of him, puffing and wiping the tears from her eyes as she tried to see his image clearly.

"Hi," she replied, taking her earphones off and holding them in her cold hands. Dan just looked at her, with her red lips and cheeks, the first of the evening snow dotting her hair.

"Baby, do you want to walk home with Daddy?" Dan said, immediately feeling Nadia's arms wrapping around his waist and holding onto him like he was the one thing that could keep her from collapsing.

"Shh, there there little one, Daddy's here. Come on, take my hand, let's get you warmed up," he said, taking off his thick felt and fur coat and wrapping it around her shoulders, instantly warming her frozen body. Nadia hadn't realized that she was frozen to her bones until the warmth of Dan's coat gave her pins and needles as she warmed up. Nadia looked at Dan, his navy business suit and tan leather satchel slung over his chest, the silver crest catching Nadia's eye.

"Daddy, what do you do?" She asked, as he loosened his crimson tie and smiled down at her.

"I'm a lawyer baby girl. I'm really impressed that you've got a big girl job," Dan said, as they walked quickly, both wanting to get out of the cold and into their dynamic in the privacy of the apartment.

"It's not that big, I just work in a store," Nadia replied, looking into the windows of the cafes they passed.

"I like that you can look after yourself," Dan said, tilting his head at the expensive activewear which Nadia was wearing. She just giggled and shrugged her shoulder as Dan opened the door to their apartment for her. Climbing the stairs, Nadia took off his coat and handed it back to him before she turned and kissed his cheek.

"Thanks, Daddy. Do you want to come in?" She asked, opening her door.

"Maybe later, but right now I think you should come into my place, let me cook for you and take care of you tonight?" He asked, making Nadia have to think for a moment. She ground her teeth before nodding and shutting her door again before turning back around to him.

"Ok," Nadia softly said, making Dan smile.

"I love that you are giving me a chance. I'll show you that you can trust me," he said opening his door and walking inside, hanging his coat and bag on the hooks at the door before turning around to see that Nadia was standing against the closed door of his apartment. He smiled, took his jacket off, followed by his tie, and walked into his bedroom.

"Do you want to have a shower or bath sweetie? I've got a few things here I think you might like," he called from his room, gaining Nadia's curiosity as she followed the sound of his voice and walked into his bedroom. Looking at the things he placed on his bed, she smiled and walked over to inspect them further.

"Did you get all these for me?" She asked, picking up the star-patterned onesie and bit her lip excitedly.

"Yeah, I wasn't sure which one you would want so I got a few. And these as well," Dan said as he half jogged to the far side of his room and opened the cupboard, taking our three pairs of thigh-high socks which matched the onesies. Nadia gasped and placed both hands on the sides of her face in surprise.

"They are all so pretty, Daddy!" Nadia squealed happily making Dan exhale in delight.

"Oh good, I took some notes from your selection. I'm pleased you like them. So now you can have a bath here because you have jammies to be changed into afterward," Dan said, sitting on the edge of the bed and looking into Nadia's sparkling eyes.

"Can you help me please, Daddy?" Nadia asked, getting stuck in her long sleeve as she tried to pull it over her head. Laughing, Dan stood up, and she held her breath as she felt his hands traced up her toned sides lifting the pink running shirt off her head, looking her gently in the eyes as he sat back down and looked at her standing in front of him in her sports tights and bra.

"Daddy, you make me nervous," Nadia said in her little voice as she began to blush. Shutting his eyes, Dan placed his hands on his knees and raised an eyebrow.

"How about now? Now I can't see you at all," he said, smiling. Nadia quickly took her sneakers and socks off before touching his hands, causing him to open one eye.

"I don't want you to laugh at me," Nadia nervously said, as she rolled her tights down.

"Why would you think I'd laugh at you little one?" Dan said frowning, his eyes filled with nothing but love.

"Because maybe you think I don't look nice," she said, making Dan tilt his head dramatically.

"Baby girl, I think you are the most beautiful girl I have ever seen!" He replied, surprised that she would be self-conscious about her appearance. Nadia had the looks of a woman most men would be too intimidated by even to approach her at a bar. She had the cold eyes that pierced a heart and a stare that rattled the most confident of men, but Dan had known her deal the minute he laid eyes on her.

"Ok, just checking," Nadia said as she stood in front of him only wearing her underwear.

"Coz like, you haven't tried anything with me. So I just don't know, like if you like me or not," Nadia said, looking down at the ground.

"Baby girl, I haven't tried anything because you're my little one. I'd rather keep all the grown-up stuff for when and if you want to have that relationship with me too. But we have only explored this side of us so, that will have to be a conversation we have when you are feeling like a big girl," Dan explained making Nadia smile and nod her head.

"Is that why you've been so nervous around me, coz you think I'm going to do grown-up things to you, little girl?" Dan asked, picking up a onesie and socks and standing up.

"Yeah," Nadia replied, excepting the hand, Dan offered her as he led her into the bathroom.

"Silly girl. I'm not like that. I like to keep both dynamics separate, I like to regress you, age play is fun too, but mostly I'll want to regress you," Dan explained as Nadia stood on the bathmat, the floor heating making the mat warm. Dan placed Nadia's things down on the wooden stool in the corner and ran the shower, wondering if he should leave or take her underwear off or what she wanted him to do.

"Daddy, I need help," Nadia said, turning around before feeling his hands unhooking the clips of her sports bra before she turned back around, letting him see her body for the first time. She slowly pulled down her panties, Dan smiling as he saw her shaved pussy and watched as she got in, under the water.

"What's for dinner, Daddy?" Nadia asked as she showered, Dan watching her model-like body twist and turn under the showerhead.

"I honestly just want a big cheesy pizza. Do

you like that? I can get you whatever you want, what do you want, baby?" Dan said, holding a towel open for Nadia who made happy noises as he dried her.

"Yeah, I like pizza, but I like mine with BBQ steak as well," she said, surprising Dan.

"Alright, we will get two pizza's then," he said, laying her on the floor, the warm tiles feeling strange under her body as she had prepared herself to be cold. Dan took a diaper and powder from the cupboard and gently slapped her thighs, waiting for her to lift up before he slid the diaper under her bottom. Sprinkling powder over her, he fastened the tabs around her body and bent down to kiss her tummy, making Nadia giggle and happily fall even deeper into her little space. She placed her thumb in her mouth as Dan dressed her in the onesie, helping Nadia to roll the sleeves up when he saw her struggle.

"I don't like things touching my wrists, Daddy," Nadia explained, keeping her leg steady as he rolled the socks up her thighs.

"I see," Dan said, sitting back on his hunches, admiring how beautiful and peaceful Nadia looked.

"But I only like long-sleeve onesies. I think the short sleeve ones are yucky," Nadia said giggling.

"Is that so?" Dan replied, picking Nadia up and holding her in his arms like a princess as he walked her through the apartment and into the living room.

"Daddy needs to have a quick shower, baby girl. I'll order our dinner, and it should be ready by the time Daddy is out of the shower, alright?" Nadia just nodded her head and swayed her legs as she sat cross-legged on the couch, waiting as Dan put on a show for her.

"I like this one, Daddy," she said, pointing to the tv as Dan put the remote down on the table.

"Alright, I'll be quick," Dan said, rushing into the shower, knowing that the pizza would be there in about 10 minutes.

Nadia watched the show with the puppies and

their exciting adventures, getting lost in the show and not hearing the first knock at the door. Dan was still in the shower as the second knock came more loudly than the first, starling Nadia and making her turn her head towards the door. As the third knock came, she quickly headed to the shower, stopping and pivoting as yet another knock came making her confused as to what to do.

"My Daddy said I can't open the door," she found herself saying, in her little voice.

"Ok, is your Daddy there? I've got your pizza here," the voice of the pizza delivery girl said on the other side of the door. Nadia just looked around nervously.

"Did he already pay online?" Nadia asked, biting her bottom lip and holding her breath.

"Um, let me see. No, he didn't. I need $20 sweetie," the woman replied, pressing her ear to the door as she heard Nadia scurry away. Nadia went to Dan's bedroom to find his wallet, opening it up and sighing in relief when she saw a 20 dollar bill. Running back to the door, Nadia pushed the note through the gap at the bottom of the door.

"There," she said happily as the woman laughed.

"Thanks, but you'll have to open the door if you want your pizza's," the woman said, making Nadia think.

"It's ok. You can leave it there. Daddy will get it later," Nadia said, running to the bathroom as she heard the shower being turned off.

"Daddy?" She said, peeping her head into the foggy bathroom.

"The pizza is here, I already paid, but she's left it out the front," Nadia said.

"Oh, baby, damn I took a lot longer than I thought I was going to," Dan said, laughing as he wrapped a blue towel around his waist and ran to the door. Opening it, he saw the pizza lady had left the pizza's on his doorstep with a note on top reading, *Sir, you need to take better care of your little girl. Leaving someone so young alone is really not on.* Dan just laughed as he scrunched the note up and threw it in the trash as he plated a slice of

Nadia's pizza for her.

"That was a close call, Daddy!" Nadia said, as she took her slice in both hands and took a huge bite.

"Mmm, yummy," she said, chewing happily, tilting her head from side to side, the happy dance she did when she ate something she enjoyed.

"I know! You were clever to get my wallet," Dan said, smiling at Nadia.

Chapter 6

Nadia had fallen asleep in Dan's arms as they had watched a film, wrapped up in blankets and full of pizza. Opening her eyes, she saw that she was still laying on his couch, but that Dan was nowhere in sight.

"Daddy?" Nadia called through the apartment, hearing a thud coming from the bedroom. Getting up slowly, she sleepily rubbed her eyes and made her way to the bedroom, smiling when she saw Dan.

"Daddy, what are you doing?" Nadia said, watching as Dan jumped around the room trying to put on his sock.

"I overslept, I'm late for work," he laughed. Nadia was happy that he wasn't angry at her, assuming it was her fault he was late.

"Oh sweetie no, it's not your fault," Dan said

as if reading her mind. Nadia just blushed, wondering if she was as obvious to everyone else as she was to Dan.

"I'll be home late today. Are you working?" Dan asked, pulling his pants up. Nadia couldn't help notice his defined muscles as he tucked his shirt into his pants and tightened his belt around his waist.

"No. Daddy, can you change me before you leave. I want to be a big girl again," Nadia asked. Dan stood still for a moment and checked his watch.

"I'm already late, an extra few minutes for my baby girl won't save me. I'm all yours," Dan said, laying Nadia down on the bed and taking her onesie off.

"But Nadia, your work out gear is still dirty," Dan said, curious as to how she would get to her apartment without clothes.

"Then it's a good thing I look so good," she said, winking at him and making Dan have to catch his breath as he saw her transform into the gorgeously seductive woman he knew her to be.

"You little tease," Dan said, looking at her naked, perfect body in front of him.

Dan opened the door to his apartment as he saw Nadia prance around, collecting her things, and coming to the door.

"It's clear," Dan said, enjoying how Nadia lived her life in extremes. Watching as Nadia quickly made her way to her door and opened it just as the elevator chimed and someone walked out. Laughing, Dan winked at Nadia who just smiled back as she slowly shut her door, locking it once it shut.

Oh my god, he's fantastic, Nadia thought to herself as she walked through her apartment, the sun streaming through the windows signaling mid-morning.

Nadia spent the day messaging with Dan. He had gotten away with being so late for work, and they had laughed at how close Nadia had been to getting caught running naked down the corridor of their apartment floor. When he had said he needed to get some work done before his boss became suspicious of his happy mood, Nadia sent him a winky smilie and put her phone in her jeans pocket before getting off the couch.

"He is a dream," she said out loud. It felt like the first time in years when she didn't have to fight herself to feel happy. It just seemed to flow through her veins.

Happiness, Nadia thought, smiling as she decided to go for a walk around the neighborhood. Putting her shoes on and grabbing her coat, she pulled the door shut behind her.
She walked passed the cafés and restaurants. She admired the window displays of the designer boutiques, and although the air was crisp, she enjoyed the warmth of the sun on her face.

"Well, now I know you are stalking me," Dan's voice laughed, making her turn around to see him. She flung her arms around his body and held him tight, nuzzling into him and smelling his cologne.

"What are you doing, lovely?" He asked, stroking her hair out of her face and kissing her forehead.

"I just thought a walk might be good. I've been inside all day," she replied, holding his hand as he led her back down the street.

"Want to get a bite to eat? I'm starving," Dan asked, Nadia just nodding her head. With him, she felt herself go into her little space with the simplest of things. Being called lovely, how he reached for her hand upon seeing her, it was those things that gave her butterflies in her stomach, but that also made her heart explode.

"Are you in the mood for something or can I pick?" He asked.

Even the way he asks still makes him sound like my Daddy, Nadia thought, resting her head on his arm as they walked.

"You can pick," she replied, laughing when they stopped at the next restaurant.

"I've picked. It's the closest one," Dan said, enjoying his decision and walked inside. It was a small sandwich joint, the smell of fries and mustard, making Nadia's stomach rumble.

"Oh, are you hungry little one?" Dan said, giving Nadia a mild heart attack. She looked around nervously, hoping that no one heard him.

"You can't call me that here," she said. Dan just smiled at her as he took her to the seats at the back.

"Are you scared someone will find out you are my beautiful baby girl?" He whispered in her ear, making her shiver.

"Yes, Daddy," Nadia replied, kissing him on the tip of his nose. Dan sat down next to her, and she snuggled into his side as they looked over the menu.

"Nadia? Nadia Harris? Is that you?" A voice said from the counter. Nadia and Dan both turned around to see a man in his mid 40's looking at Nadia. He was a tall man and looked like someone on the Forbes billionaire list. His short grey hair complimented by the navy business suit he wore. Nadia froze, and Dan could feel her heart skip a beat as she looked at the man like a deer in headlights.

"I think you must be mistaken," Dan said, trying to get the man to leave.

"No, I know it's you. I would remember those lips anywhere," the man said, coming over to stand over Nadia, sandwiching her between him and Dan.

"Well, aren't you going to introduce me? I thought I taught you better than that?" The man said, enjoying the discomfort he brought to Nadia. Nadia just looked at the ground, making the man laugh and extend his hand to Dan.

"I'm Rupert, Rupert Sullivan. Nadia and I use to, well, what did we use to do, baby?" Rupert said, making Dan tighten his grip around the older man's hand. Letting go, Dan stood up, meeting the Rupert at eye level.

"You'd better go. It is clear Nadia doesn't want to see you," Dan said, moving Nadia, so she was behind him.

"Well, a baby doesn't know what she wants,

that's why she needs Daddy to tell her," Rupert said, laughing as a tear escaped Nadia's eye. Rupert turned around, collected his order, and left the restaurant, Dan watching him with protective viciousness in his eyes until he was out of sight. Sitting back down, Dan saw that their meal had arrived and Nadia sat frozen in the booth.

"Talk to me sweetie," Dan said, bringing her close as she suddenly burst into tears. He held her, stroked her hair and waited until she pushed him away, looking up at Dan with the saddest eyes he had ever seen.

"I don't want to," Nadia slowly said, looking at the delicious food in front of her and beginning to eat in silence. Dan just looked at her, and although he wanted to have his questions answered, he didn't push the issue with her and bit into his wrap.

Dan paid for the meal, and they left the restaurant, silence, and questions still looming in the air. They had walked a block before Dan looked at Nadia as they waited for the street light to turn green.

"I get that you don't want to talk about it, I just want you to know that whatever that was back there, you aren't losing me," Dan said, feeling Nadia reach for his hand.

"Thanks," she replied, walking across the road, Dan's hand making her feel safe.

"I wouldn't even know where to start," she said, pointing to a park bench, not wanting to go home to sit in her apartment alone. Dan let her lead as she found the bench she liked and sat down. They sat there, watching the world spin around them, Nadia feeling as though she was invisible.

"When I was 18 I ran away from home because it was just too dangerous to be there any longer," Nadia began, remembering how she had learned the hard way to lock herself in the bathroom when her father's friends had come over to drink. Shaking her head, wanting the memory to be gone, she tried to form the words her heart so desperately wanted to speak.

"I ran out of money pretty quickly. I bounced from couch to couch but pretty soon I was on the streets. He found me," Nadia said, feeling the sting of his name on the tip of her tongue. Dan wrapped his arm around Nadia who curled into him, placing her legs over his as she watched the trees in the park rustle.

"Pretty soon I was turning tricks from him, his friends would come over, and I'd be their entertainment. He gave me a place to live, clothes, food. I didn't know how to leave him. So he left me instead," Nadia said, swinging her leg, kicking a stone back and forth as she waited for Dan's reply. She looked up at him, hoping that he still liked her as saw the anger in his face.

"I can't believe some people. I am so sorry that happened to you," he said, making her exhale and rest her head on his arm.

"He was my first Daddy. I didn't know what I was doing, and he was so abusive and cruel. Then one day, I woke up to my bags packed at the door with a note on them saying that if I was still there when he got back, he would call the police," she continued to explain.

"So I just left. I tried to call him, but he had blocked my number, I tried to find him, but when I went back the next day, someone else was moving into his house, and they said that he had left town. I was all on my own again," Nadia said, biting her bottom lip as she tried to hold her tears back.

"I've got you now, darling, and I won't let anything bad happen to you. You'll see," Dan said. Nadia thought she would feel better after sharing her story with Dan, but as they got up to leave, her vision became blurry, a sweat broke out on her forehead, and the color drained from her face as she lunged forward and was sick behind the park bench.

"It's ok, Daddy is here, let it out sweetie," Dan lovingly said as he rubbed her back. Nadia's eyes watered as her stomach emptied itself of the meal she had only just consumed almost as if her body was trying to cleanse itself from the memory she had just dragged up.

"Daddy's got you, come on, baby girl, let me take you home," Dan said, taking out a tissue from his pocket and stopping a peddler and buying Nadia a bottle of water before they left the park.

Chapter 7

Nadia had stayed in bed for five days after seeing Rupert. Dan had been by her side almost the whole time, only going into work once during the week. He had watched her as she slept, her nightmares reoccurring as she relived her past in her dreams.

"It's just a bad dream, little one," Dan said, as Nadia began to stir in her sleep violently. Dan gently shook her awake, holding her hand as she gasped, her eyes popping open, and her heart beating wildly.

"Shh, Daddy is here. You're safe, and nobody is going to hurt you," he said, as she began to cry. She hated this. Not being able to shake the demons that had haunted her for so long they had become a part of who she was. She didn't want to be like this. She wanted to be happy. To be able to love Dan the way she wanted to, freely, without fear of him hurting her or turning on her. She knew in her mind that she could trust him, but her heart was the thing which ruled her life and just like every other time, she felt uncomfortable, it said to run.

"I'm sorry you don't have to be here. I can handle this. I know you've missed a lot of things this week because of me," Nadia said, only stopping because of the paci Dan put in her mouth.

"Shh, little girl. Don't talk about such silly things. You are more important than the jerks at my office," Dan replied, putting a cold towel on Nadia's forehead and patting her left side until she was back asleep.

The following Monday, Nadia got up before Dan, stretching her toes along the wooden floors before walking into the kitchen. This was the first time she had been out of bed for a reason other than using the bathroom. Walking to the coffee machine, she turned it on and waited for the creamy warm liquid to fill her cup. Taking it, she went to sit down on the couch and listened to the birds chirping outside. Closing her eyes, she wondered who she would have been if she had been given a different life. She had longed for someone to rescue her, to save her, and every time someone tried, all she did was push them away. She was grateful to herself for not pushing Dan away. She liked how he had calmed her wild heart, and she loved even more that she let him.

How did I get so lucky, Nadia thought as she saw him run around the corner, worry on his face.

"Baby?!" Dan said, checking her over to make sure everything was alright.

"Daddy?!" Nadia playfully replied. She looked up at him and waited for him to speak.

"Are you ok?" He asked, sitting down next to her when she nodded yes.

"I was worried when you weren't in bed. Why didn't you wake me?" Dan asked, seeing that her coffee cup was empty and placing it on the table.

"Because you've been working overtime on

me and I wanted you to rest, Daddy," she replied, kissing his cheek.

"Such a sweet girl. Can I get you breakfast?" He asked, already knowing what Nadia would like.

"Waffles!" Nadia happily yelled, lifting her arms in the air and getting cuddled by Dan.

"Hey, Nadia?" Dan said, using her name to signal that he wanted to have an adult conversation with her. She just cleared her throat and wriggled from his arms.

"Dan," she replied, suddenly becoming the alpha female he had seen a handful of times.

"I think, maybe going to therapy and getting some professional help for this might be a good idea," he said, catching her off guard.

"Therapy is for people with problems. I don't have problems," she replied, taking the ingredients from the pantry to make waffles. Dan just made himself an espresso and raised an eyebrow at her.

"Fine, I have a slight problem. But I think I'm good now," Nadia said, wanting to end this conversation. Dan just took her hand gently in his and gripped it tightly when she tried to pull away.

"What if I come with you?" He suggested making her roll her eyes.

"What I want to do more than not go to therapy would be to have you there. How creepy, I don't want you to know all this shit, to begin with. Just drop it," Nadia said, hoping that by rejecting Dan's suggestion, she wouldn't lose him.

"I'll drop it, once you go," he said, kissing the tip of her nose and making her laugh and groan knowing that she'd be making that appointment sooner rather than later.

"How is everything going?" Her therapist asked, two days later. Nadia had avoided eye contact for as long as possible, something about the way this therapist looked at her made her feel, seen, and that was deeply uncomfortable.

"Really great," Nadia lied behind a smile.

She can probably figure out I'm lying, look at the way she's staring at me like she already knows,

Nadia thought, looking around the room and not knowing where she was meant to start. Her therapist looked at her expectantly, reading through the front Nadia was so desperately trying to keep from falling.

"Really?" She asked, raising an eyebrow and making Nadia just laugh at her futile attempt actually to be alright.

"No, obviously, I'm sitting here," she said gesturing to the room.

"So why have you come today?" The therapist said. Nadia looked around the room, wondering how fast an hour could go.

"Because my boyfriend said I probably should," Nadia replied, excited to be able to call Dan her boyfriend.

"Why do you think he suggested it?" the woman asked.

Oh great, she's persistent, Nadia thought, annoyed that she was going to have to give this woman something to go with.

"I don't know because I had a rough start?"

Nadia said hoping that was enough.

"Tell me about it," the woman said, causing Nadia to breathe loudly.

"I don't want to," Nadia replied, annoyed that her guard was being taken down so quickly by this stranger with a look on her face like she knew all of Nadia's secrets.

She's got, like super fucking powers or something, she angrily thought, looking at the ground.

"Look, I know you are trying to help and just doing your job, but I really don't want to be here," Nadia said looking at her dead in the eye, slightly unnerved by the unwavering stare she was receiving back. Breaking first, Nadia looked away, annoyed that she didn't feel in control anymore.

"I know you don't want to, but tell me what happened anyway," the woman said, smiling at Nadia, challenging her to be brave. Nadia just smiled a sideward smile, rolled her eyes, and gave a half-laugh, surprised that she suddenly didn't completely hate being in the room and sighed. She bit her bottom lip, annoyed that tears escaped her eyes like a flood breaking as she breathed deeply trying to hold them back.

"It's ok, you're safe here, I'm not going to hurt you," the woman said only making Nadia laugh and shake her head in disbelief as she wiped her tears away.

You probably would have, given the chance. You're probably just like they were. You're all the same. But I'd fucking kill you if you tried now though...or, would I? She thought to herself, seriously contemplating which decision she would make, glad she hadn't let that slip from her lips.

"My father was an abusive drunk. I don't have a mother, and I was homeless when I was 18," Nadia said in one breath, leaning back into the couch. Feeling the roughly put together scabs of her heart being slowly ripped off and the wounds made vulnerable, exposed and bleeding, a pain almost unbearable to allow herself to feel.

Well, that was different, Nadia said on her

walk home. The therapist had said words Nadia didn't know the meaning of and she spent the whole 20-minute walk doing internet search after internet search learning about energy, NLP, and the different levels of hypnotherapy. Walking into Dan's apartment, she put her phone on the kitchen bench and upon seeing him, wrapped her arms around him, kissing him on the mouth.

"Woah, what was that for," he said, surprised at her sudden passion.

"I'm pretty sure this is what happy feels like," Nadia replied, going to the fridge and taking out two beers.

"And I'm also pretty sure I'm about to be drunk," she added, opening both bottles, turning on a country playlist which boomed through the apartment and walked back over to him.

"So it was good then?" Dan asked, as the timer of the dino nuggets chimed, Nadia raising an eyebrow, putting her beer down.

"What's in there?" She suddenly asked, already knowing the answer. Dan just laughed.

"You don't have to have them if you don't want, I just wasn't sure how you'd be when you came back, so I thought it was better to be prepared," he explained. Nadia looked at the beer in her hand and the tray of nuggets in Dan's and just moaned.

"I don't know what I want either!" She said in destress.

"Look, finish the beer, then have the nuggies, and then I'll get you ready for bed, ok?" Dan suggested, Nadia just nodding as she chugged her drink, finishing it before Dan came over with her plate.

"Heaven," she said, happily sighing and eating with her eyes closed.

"I'm glad it was so good, baby," Dan said, taking the beer bottle away and watched as she happy danced as she ate.

"I wonder how long this will last?" Nadia asked when Dan came to sit down next to her.

"What do you mean?" He questioned, pulling her into his lap and smiling at her as she turned in his arms.

"I just hope that this awesome feeling doesn't go away," Nadia said, burying her face into Dan's chest, snuggling with him as he turned off the music and turned on a show.

Nadia knew that she had to go to work the next day, and groaned as her alarm woke her up.

"I just don't think this is normal to be woken up by that noise," she complained as she got up and walked through her apartment, turning on the coffee machine, making a piece of toast and eating it with her eyes closed. She had spent the night in her own apartment, Dan staying in his. She had said that she wanted to see if she could manage a night without him but had tossed and turned the whole night. Unbeknownst to Nadia, Dan had suffered the same fate. She beamed when a knock came from her door, assuming it would be Dan. Opening it excitedly, Nadia dropped her piece of toast when she saw the image that greeted her.

"Hey bunny," Rupert said, standing in front

of her making her forget she was a thriving 27-year-old with a resume that screamed success and abundance. She forgot that she had a man who loved her, she forgot that she had somehow managed to survive all her hardest days and in an instant, she was back there, the girl she had worked so hard to distance herself from.

"Well, aren't you going to let me in? Daddy wants to see how far his good girl has come," Rupert said, stepping forward, making Nadia step back and hold her breath.

"Um, no," she said, the words sounding more like a suggestion than a command making Rupert laugh.

"No? When have you ever said no? I don't remember ever saying that *no* was an option," he said trying to push his way in, Nadia refusing to move. She tensed her calves, reached up and pushed him back, not moving him an inch.

"You'll have to do better than that," he said, lifting his hand to strike her, backhanding her across her face. She let out a high pitched gasp as she fell to the ground, Rupert standing over her, his hands on the front of his belt buckle. Nadia closed her eyes, wishing she could disappear, wishing that she wasn't crying, wishing that he would go away as Dan's door opened.

"The fuck?" Dan said, quickly taking in the situation, dropping his briefcase, placing his hand on Rupert's shoulder and turning him around, ducking the punch Rupert threw before Dan slammed his fist up under Rupert's chin, knocking him back and causing him to cough. Dan's eyes burned with a violence Nadia didn't know he could possess as he walked toward Rupert, blocking his punches and tripping him, straddling his chest and laying his fists into the older mans face until Rupert couldn't open his eyes. His blood spraying across the floor as Dan grabbed the sides of his face only to smash his head back against the floor. Getting up, Rupert unconscious on the floor, Dan went to Nadia who had stood and rested against the wall, having watched the whole thing.

"Baby girl, let Daddy see," Dan said,

becoming the gentle, loving man Nadia knew him to be.

"You're cut, baby, come inside and let me look after that for you," Dan said, picking up his briefcase and placing it just inside his door, before going back and dragging Rupert's body into the corridor and leaving him there.

"I had no idea you could fight like that," Nadia quietly said, as she sat on his kitchen bench and let him put ointment on her cheek.

"I watched my father beat my mother, and I watched her choose him over herself and me every time. She was weak and broken. I told myself I would never be that pathetic, lying to herself about why she should put up with such a crappy life. And as much as I can understand her reasons, hell, I can even understand his reasons for being such a prick, I decided that I needed to heal myself so that I didn't become either of them. I learned how to defend myself early. Then I learned how to love, out of everything, that was the hard part. Something neither of them managed to learn how to do," Dan explained as he placed a bandaid over Nadia's cut.

"There, little one," he said, kissing her forehead and helping her get down.

"I can't go to work like this," Nadia said, attempting to pull the bandaid off.

"Then don't. Let's just, retire. Go do something else. Live a different life. There is nothing particularly interesting about my job. I hate how they take their pound of flesh and give nothing back," Dan said. It was these moments that made Nadia know she loved him. Who else would burn the world down with her until it matched a dream they carried in their hearts.

"Fuck it. I've got some savings. Do you? How long could you go without work?" Nadia said, looking down and realizing that she was still wearing her pajamas. Dan sat on the floor and kicked off his shoes, making Nadia laugh at how he looked with his elegant suit and fancy hair cut, sitting on the floor. Joining him, she crawled into his lap as he took out his phone and dialed a number.

"God, I hadn't registered that I've been waiting for this day. I've got savings too, could probably go about a year without work," he said before quickly becoming serious.

"Good morning, Mark. I'm really sorry, actually, no, I'm not. I'm fucking over the moon to tell you that I won't be coming into work, um, ever again. I quit," Dan said, hanging up the phone and sighing with relief, laying back on the floor and bringing Nadia with him. Breathing as though he had just run a race, Dan's eyes watered, and he let his tears fall from his eyes.

"Thank you, baby girl," he said, kissing her and holding her tight as he relaxed into the floor.

Chapter 8

Dan and Nadia stayed like that until their bodies became numb. Nadia ringing her work and quitting as well. Looking at each other, they both laughed and shook their heads in disbelief.

"Did we actually just do that?!" Nadia squealed, clapping her hands excitedly and jumping up and down.

"I feel free. I hadn't even realized that I had felt so caged. Oh my god, we can do whatever the fuck we want, baby!" He replied, going to the cupboard and pouring a whiskey. Nadia tilted her head left and right, before walking into the kitchen.

"What? There are no rules now. I don't have to turn up to work dead sober, I don't have to wear this fucking leash ever again," Dan said as he loosened the tie around his neck and ripped it from his body. Nadia took the bottle from his hand and took a deep swing, gasping as the liquid burned her throat.

"I don't have to be nice to rude jerks who think that treating retail staff like shit makes them special," Nadia said, placing the bottle down.

"Wanna get day drunk?" Dan said, pouring another glass.

"I kinda think I already am," Nadia laughed as she turned on music and danced around the kitchen.

"But seriously, what do you want to do now?" She asked, stopping suddenly and sitting on the floor. Dan came over with blank paper and the crayons she kept on his office desk and sat down with her.

"Let's design our life," Dan said, sitting next to Nadia who took the pink crayon.

"I kinda like my therapist. She's not what I expected. I'd like to keep seeing her. I think I've still got some stuff to sort out," Nadia said writing that down. Dan just nodded and thought about what he wanted.

"I want to own a bar. I wanted to learn about hospitality until like, I got told not too. Fuck, why did we even listen to anyone but ourselves?" He asked, shaking his head.

"Oh, that's original, a Daddy with a bar. There's actually a bar for sale next to the sandwich store we went to that time. The owner is only selling because he is moving to Jersey," Nadia said, writing down the bar idea next to the therapist.

"So we want to stay in the city?" Dan asked, smiling when Nadia nodded.

"I like it here, you?" She asked, Dan, agreeing eagerly.

"Great. Well, I guess we are moving in together?" Nadia asked, biting her bottom lip and smiling excitedly.

"One thousand percent," Dan said, opening his phone to look at houses for sale.

"I will sell this place. Do you rent or own yours?" He asked, taking an orange crayon and writing *house.*

"I'd like to frame this when we rebuild our lives," Nadia laughed, drawing a picture of a house.

"And I rent it, so that's easy for me. I'll just break the lease," she added, shrugging a shoulder.

"Damn, we are actually doing this," Dan happily said, leaning over and kissing Nadia passionately.

"I think I should go get changed. And maybe clean the blood up from my floor," Nadia said, standing up and stretching.

"Yeah, sorry about that. I'll help," Dan said, following her to the door, glad to see that Rupert was gone. Nadia opened her door and saw the dark smear across the wooden floors.

"It'll be easy, you go get dressed, I'll get started," Dan said, seeing Nadia becoming uncomfortable with the scene.

"Thanks," she whispered, heading into her bedroom, Dan getting to work right away. He pulled out bleach from her cleaning cupboard and decided to use his shirt as a rag to clean it up.

"It's not like I'll be needing this one

anymore," he happily said, mopping up the mess, his muscled body flexing as he did so.

"Huh, that was quick," he said out loud just as Nadia came back out of the room.

"Oh, wow. I had thought it would take longer. It always takes so long in the movies," she said, turning on the coffee machine.

"I was thinking. Maybe I don't want to own that bar. I think I'd like to live by the beach," Dan said, throwing his shirt in the bin.

"Yeah, same. I'll just do skype sessions with my therapist. Ever notice that therapist has a really unfortunate word in it? Let's go somewhere new," Nadia agreed, pouring sugar into her cup.

"I can't believe how much has changed in two hours," she laughed, sipping the drink.

"Yeah, right?" Dan agreed, shaking his head and sighing contentedly, closing his eyes and falling asleep, Nadia coming to join him, cuddling into him and falling asleep on his chest.

"Baby, wake up darling," Dan said, gently

rocking Nadia in his arms. The world had continued to spin around then while they had slept, the sun replaced by the moon the next time Dan had opened his eyes again.

"Huh?" Nadia asked, slowly blinking as she adjusted to the reality she now witnessed.

"What's the time?" She asked, laughing when she saw how dark the room was.

"8:30, we slept for the whole day," Dan said, his voice hoarse.

"Wow. Want to go to the movies?" Nadia asked, smiling in the dark, the moonlight which came through the windows outlining her form as she stood.

"Why not. It's not like we have to get up early in the morning," Dan said, cracking his back and yawning before turning on the light.

"Tomorrow I want to go to the real estate and sort out how to put my place on the market for tenants," he said, Nadia nodding her head.

"Ok, I'm just going to have a shower," Nadia said, walking to the bathroom, Dan following, wanting to see her body.

"Are you going just to stand there watching me?" She asked, Dan nodding, the toothy grin Nadia liked spreading across his face.

"Then put a song on," she instructed, causing Dan to raise his eyebrow.

"Please, Daddy," Nadia seductively added, waiting for the music to start.

"Um, probs not that one," she laughed as Dan played some metal song she had stopped liking years ago. Changing it to something more smooth, Dan gasped as he saw Nadia begin to dance.

"I had no idea you could move like that," he said, pulling the chair Nadia had in the corner over and sitting down.

"I've got a few tricks you're yet to learn of," she said, her hips rolling slowly, her eyes locking onto his, her hands moving over her body. She danced for Dan, enjoying how he looked at her like she held the answers to all his questions — sitting back down when she shook her head when he tried to come into the shower with her.

"I love you, Daddy," Nadia said, turning the water off and accepting the towel Dan passed her. Stopping the music, Dan just gulped.

"Please don't feel like you have to say that, I'm not going anywhere, you know that right?" He asked, drying Nadia's body.

"Do you really think I'd say it if I didn't mean it?" She whispered in his ear, giving him goosebumps.

"Alright, enough of that," he laughed, trying to get away from the closeness he felt his heart getting to Nadia's.

"No, stay here. Stay with me," she said, seeing the fear in his eyes.

"I'm not going to hurt you either," she added, looking up at him.

"I guess it has to go both ways, huh?" Dan said, trying to keep his heart open and connected to hers. Nadia nodded her head and refused to look away from him, a trick she had learned from her therapist, Dan matching her gaze with equal intensity.

"How did I get so lucky?" He asked, smiling vulnerably down on Nadia, feeling small and wondering if this is how Nadia felt all the time. Nadia just shrugged her shoulder, making him laugh and look at his watch.

"We will miss the movie if we don't get going," he said, Nadia, quickly running to the bedroom.

"What am I going to wear, Daddy?" Nadia called, waiting for him to come into the room.

"Let me see," Dan said, opening her cupboard and flicking through her clothes.

"These," Dan said, throwing a pair of black jeans on top of Nadia making her giggle.

"And this," he added, throwing her bra onto the bed next, followed by an old band t-shirt.

"Really?!" Nadia asked, getting covered in her black leather jacket with the black fur lining landing on her next.

"Yeah, what's wrong with that?" Dan asked, taking out her combat boots and pink socks from the top shelf and placing them down next to the bed.

"Nothing, now that I have my pink sockies," Nadia said, wiggling her toes into them as Dan helped her get dressed.

"Ok, now that you are all done, Daddy needs to get ready," Dan said, taking her hand and leading her out of her apartment and into his.

"I'll just be a moment," Dan said, as Nadia began to raid his fridge.

"We will get food out, bubba," he yelled from the bathroom hearing her open a packet of chips.

"That's fine, I'll eat these too though," she giggled to herself as she crunched on the potato chips.

They walked out onto the street 30 minutes later, hand in hand, feeling as though they had finally solved all their problems. Smiling up at Dan, Nadia squeezed his hand tighter in happiness, skipping along next to him. It was 10 o'clock, and Nadia loved how they took the back streets to the cinema. The full moon lit their path, and Dan stood taller than everyone who passed them, making Nadia feel safe and protected. They ordered tapas at the cinema restaurant and popcorn and ice cream when they bought their tickets before walking into the dark theatre. Sitting down quickly, Dan passed Nadia her popcorn and laughed as she became instantly perplexed on the big screen, kissing her on her forehead as she munched on the salty snack.

"This is a really good movie," Nadia tried to whisper but speaking in a loud hissing instead making Dan laugh.

"Shh, baby," he replied, settling into the seat and watching the film.

"Oh, you look sleepy, little one," Dan said as they exited the cinema. It was past midnight, and seeing Nadia clutch his arm nervously being out so late, he waited by the lights of the cinema entrance for a taxi, hailing for it as he saw the yellow vehicle approach. Giving the driver directions to his apartment, Dan wrapped his arm around Nadia who rested her head on his chest, closing her eyes and feeling herself fall asleep and falling into a dream about the girl in the tree. The girl with the dirt on her knees and hands, her hair falling out of her ponytail and her denim overalls with the tear on the thigh.

"What are you doing here?" Nadia heard herself saying to the girl who just laughed. "What do you mean? I live here! Maybe I should ask you the same question? You haven't visited me in forever!" The girl dramatically replied before giggling and jumping from the branch she was sitting on to one which was higher up the tree.

"Wait!" Nadia called, desperately trying to climb the tree to find the place where the girl was now sitting, swinging her legs over the edge and looking curiously at Nadia who finally reached the branch.

"You didn't use to take so long to climb up here," the girl said. Nadia just rolled her eyes as she sat next to the girl and looked out over the cityscape that greeted her eyes.

"As you said, it's been a while," Nadia said, taking in the view.

"Did you forget about me?" The girl said, having never taken her eyes off Nadia.

"What? No. Of course not, why would you say that?" Nadia angrily said, looking down at the girl who just raised an eyebrow at her.

"Yeah, you did. Just own it. You forgot about me. And now the question is, what are you going to do about it?" She challenged making Nadia scoff and look back out over the city. She saw the lights of the street flicker. She saw the red and white lights of the cars on the roads moving around the city like blood in its veins. She saw how Dan walked out of the apartment, and she saw herself run into his arms. Smiling, Nadia watched like a movie how they walked up their street, her heart full and saw how he passed her the lead of a big dog with a thick fluffy coat of black fur.

"Looks like you have everything you ever

wanted," the girl in the tree said, reaching out to place her hand over Nadia's.

"Yeah. So why do I still feel like this?" Nadia said, looking at the girl with tears in her eyes. The girl just took an envelope from her overall pocket. A drawing on ripped paper, the pieces having been taped together.

"You've never let me see this before," Nadia said, looking at the drawing she held in her hands. The picture she had ripped up herself when she had given it to her Father only to have him cruelly laugh at it and let it drop to the floor before walking out of the room.

"You did a good job of this actually. I really like how you made the sun so bright," Nadia said.

"He was really just such a jerk not to like it. Look at how pretty you made the house," Nadia said, repositioning herself as the girl sat on her lap.

"Really?" The girl asked, snuggling into Nadia. Nadia wrapped her arms around the girl and kissed her forehead as the girl began to cry.

"I won't forget about you again. I'm sorry I

did," Nadia whispered, the girl sucking her thumb as she just nodded her head and curled into Nadia.

"I've got you. You're alright," Nadia said, as she woke up, realizing that she was sucking her thumb, her cheeks wet with tears.

"You were crying in your sleep, baby," Dan said, his face full of concern. The taxi driver was collecting the change to give to Dan, and Nadia closed her eyes, wanting to be back in the tree, but the dream was gone.

"Yeah, fine," Nadia said as she got out of the taxi and made her way up the front steps of their apartment.

Chapter 9

"Are you going to tell me what you were dreaming about?" Dan asked as they entered his apartment. Nadia was tired, more psychologically than anything else and she just frowned at Dan who put both his hands up in defense.

"Or it can wait till morning," he quickly added, getting a faint smile from Nadia who dropped onto the couch.

"Oh no, baby girl, come on, don't fall asleep there," he said, walking over to her and picking her up before carrying her to the bedroom. Placing her down gently, he took her clothes off, receiving zero assistance from Nadia who closed her eyes and smiled as she felt Dan pull the sheets back and wrap her in her favorite pink blankets.

"Daddy," Nadia said, reaching for him, opening her eyes when she couldn't find him.

"Where are you?" She asked, wriggling out the warm cocoon Dan had settled her in and walking to the sound of Dan in the kitchen.

"I should have known you wouldn't have stayed where I left you. I'm just getting something to eat," Dan said, making a sandwich, offering Nadia bite, secretly glad when she declined.

"What are we even doing? We haven't even had a conversation about any of this, not really. We just kept coming up with ideas that we both liked that sound of," Nadia said, walking back to the bedroom with Dan. Going to the bathroom to clean their teeth before snuggling back in bed, Dan making Nadia her cocoon once more.

"Ok, let's have a conversation in the morning, little one," Dan said already half asleep. The nap Nadia had in the back of the taxi had done her wonders as she opened the window next to her side of the bed and counted the few stars that managed to shine out against the lights which light up the city. Letting her mind wander, she slipped into the memory of her dream. Nadia remembered wearing those overalls, how the dirt had gotten on her knees when she played football with the boys — tackling the boy who ran off and cried to his Mama because she got the ball off him.

"Loser," she said out loud thinking about him, the same smirk she had on her face then, re-emerging on her face in the darkroom she now lay in. She remembered how she had snuck into her teacher's art cupboard at school to steal the crayons she used to draw the picture for her Father. A girl in her class had caught her, which meant that Nadia had to confront her teacher. Nadia had straight-faced lied her ass off, following the only rule she ever listened to which was to deny till death. She'd been taught that one from her Father when the cops had come around to their house after someone had been shot on their front porch. She remembered the time she had slashed another teacher's tires when she had gotten in trouble, deciding that one wasn't enough.

"Fuck them all," she had said out loud as she dug the knife into the rubber, ripping the air out of them as though she was gutting a pig. Smiling, Nadia closed her eyes and turned into Dan, who opened his arms in his sleep and pulled her in close sighing happily in his sleep.

"Ok, let's do this properly," Dan said the next morning. He had set Nadia up in the corner of the living room, and she was busy coloring in a picture in the coloring in book he had bought her the previous week on his way home from work. He had gone into a toy store when the window display had caught his eye. The big pink and purple teddy bears on either side of the side large Ferris wheel in the middle of the window had candy in each of the carriages, but it was the blinking fairy lights that lined the bottom that sold him as he walked inside. Looking for both the pink and purple teddy bears, he bought those as well as a coloring in book that came with tubes of colored glitter. The glitter had been a hit, with Nadia using it for special pictures that Dan had proudly put on his fridge, after swearing black and blue that nothing would ever be put on there. He had one of the new model fridges that had a large touch screen on the front. Although he knew that he could take a photo of the adorable artworks that Nadia made for him, and display a photo of them on the screen, Dan loved the way Nadia's face had lit up when he had used sticky tape to secure the drawing. Dan was planning to take her shopping the next day to buy magnets, but he liked how rustic the tape looked.

"Ok, Daddy here is a list of things I've decided you need to do for me every day," Nadia said, giggling hysterically at her joke. Dan just chuckled as he walked over to where she was sitting and put her plate of star-shaped watermelon down in front of her, taking the coloring book away.

"Oh, thank you, Daddy," Nadia said, clapping her hands and opening her mouth. Dan placed a star in her mouth, and she ate happily while Dan read over her list. He laughed and took out her red crayon, and she instantly knew that her demands would not be met.

"No Daddy, they are non-negotiables," Nadia laughed, receiving another star.

"Getting extra treats because your teddies need treats too is non-negotiable?" Dan asked, making Nadia laughed as she rolled onto her back.

"Ok, let's be serious," Dan said, being serious, Nadia sitting up not wanting to annoy him.

"Ok," she said, still feeling little but being able to have this conversation.

"First of all, I already think we have a great handle on what you love and hate and I think that we have a really good balance of adult and baby time, what do you think?" Dan asked Nadia, nodding enthusiastically, and finishing her breakfast.

"I think the thing we need to discuss is, punishments," she said before hiding under her blanket.

"I don't ever want to punish you. What do you think our rules should be. You're already such a good girl, I can't imagine you doing something naughty," Dan said, making Nadia burst out laughing.

"You wait, I'm only perfect right now because I don't want to lose you," Nadia said giggling and coming out from under her blankie.

"Is that so?!" Dan asked, already knowing that it was the truth. Nodding, Nadia thought while Dan spoke.

"Ok, so rules. I'd like you to keep going for a run every second day, you always seem so happy when you go and so moody when you don't. You'll be Daddy's good girl at night, let me get you ready for bed, but during the day I'd like you to be a big girl unless I tell you otherwise. I still want you to call me Daddy and let me choose things for you like ordering at restaurants. And before you start to tell me no, don't worry I'll make sure I only order you things you actually like, I'm not mean!" Dan said when he saw Nadia put out that he wanted to order for her.

"Ok, but only the things I like," she said, making a point of this rule.

"Regarding punishments, what sort of thing

would you think suitable?" Dan asked, writing down notes as they spoke. Nadia thought, deciding that she'd enjoy spankings too much for them to be a punishment.

"I think something gross like, I have to eat only boiled vegetables for dinner, or I don't get an allowance for a week would be things I really didn't like. I'd just get turned on if you spanked me, Daddy," Nadia explained, Dan taking notes.

"So, if I bent you over my knee and pulled down your panties just to make your little ass red you'd find that hot?" Dan teased, grabbing at Nadia who giggled and playfully pushed him away, nodding her head and looking at him with innocent eyes.

"Noted," Dan said, stopping when he saw Nadia begin to regress. He cleared his throat and got up, taking her hand and pulling her to her feet.

"I think we have more than enough to go on sweetheart. How about we go for a drive, there is a really lovely place on the other side of town I'd love to take you too," Dan said, Nadia, following him to his room, sucking her thumb.

Nadia had been surprised that Dan wanted her to be his baby girl in public so quickly, and rolled around his bed as he diapered and dressed her. He had picked a puffy diaper, pink fluffy diaper cover and a white pinafore dress which made her breasts stand out. She had helped him by holding her feet still as he had put on her ankle socks and pink low-cut Converse sneakers before he took her hair out and placed a pink, glitter headband with a bow in her hair.

"Beautiful," he said, lifting her skirt and feeling the soft material of her diaper cover, making her giggle and push his hands away.

"Daddy, you're so silly," she said, blushing and turning away from him.

"One more thing," he said, taking out a pink pacifier and placing it in her mouth, exciting Nadia as she happily sucked on the big rubber nipple. Dan kissed her forehead, and he went to get dressed, coming back, and making Nadia's eyes go wide.

"You're pretty Daddy," she said when she saw his dark denim jeans, white long sleeve pullover and camel-colored cable knit cardigan with the sleeve rolled up. He smiled before scooping Nadia up and carrying to his car, happy that he wasn't as work as he buckled her into the passenger seat.

"Where are we going, Daddy?" Nadia asked as they drove out onto the road. Dan's big SVU roared into life as hit on the acceleration pedal, making Nadia laugh.

"There's this place that I heard about which is like a café designed for people in the community. I thought it might be nice to check it out together. Would you be interested in that? We can always go somewhere else if you aren't," Dan said but knowing Nadia's answer by the excitement in her eyes.

"Oh my god, yes please, Daddy. Let's go there," Nadia said, clapping her hands. She looked out the window and watched as they headed out of town and into a more suburban setting, confirming the belief Nadia held that the quiet streets in tree-lined suburbs were where all the really kinky people lived.

"We are almost there little one. If I'm wrong and this place sucks, we can leave straight away," Dan said, taking Nadia's hand in his as he drove off-road and down what looked like forest on either side of them.

"This is kinda scary," Nadia said, taking her pacifier out and looking out of the windows as they were suddenly driving on a black stone-paved road. Dan and Nadia both gasped at what they saw as the trees faded and what resembled a town emerged. In the middle of the dense forest which surrounded the property, what resembled a town had been built. There was a main street with middle-street parking, shops on either side. A toy store, multiple cafés, and restaurants, an ice cream shop, and bar and lounge were all on one side of the street, and as Dan made a U-turn to drive down the other side, Nadia turned to look at him in astonishment.

"Daddy, what is this place?!" She exclaimed as she saw the picnic area with the adult baby play equipment.

"I can't believe it either. I guess it's more than just a café. Let's park and go check it out," Dan said. As they drove to find a park, they both watched the people who moved about the street. Daddies and Mommies of all different styles looked after their littles, and she reached for Dan's hand.

"Who would work in these stores?" Nadia said to Dan, who unbuckled his seat belt. Getting out the car and coming around to her side, he undid her belt and took her from the truck.

"I guess people in the community, baby girl," Dan replied, still looking around in a daze. It was one thing to create a play space in their apartments, but this was public, open, a space where he could apparently bend Nadia over his knee and spank her ass without anyone batting an eyelid, as he saw a Mommy doing to her naughty boy.

"Are you still hungry? Let's go get some lunch," Dan said, pulling on Nadia's hand slightly as he walked with her to the closest restaurant. Going inside, he was just as surprised as he had been before with the sights which greeted him. There, Mommies were breastfeeding their littles, and littles colored in at the table while their Daddies talked and joked over steak sandwiches and beer. Caregivers spoon-feeding their babies or holding a bottle to their lips while they waited for their meal to be made, made Dan wonder how he had never heard of this whole place before. He took Nadia to one of the tables by the front window and sat down.

"This might be my favorite place in the whole world, Daddy!" Nadia exclaimed in a hushed squeal.

"I love it too," he replied as a mid-twenty-year-old woman approached the table.

"Hey, is it your first time here or do you know how our ordering system works?" She warmly asked.

"It's our first time," Dan replied, accepting the menus the woman gave him.

"Ok so, you can order from the menu directly. Or you can go over there and get the chief to create whatever you'd like from the fresh, locally sourced ingredients," the bubbly woman said. Nadia wondered how this place advertised for staff, deciding that she didn't care when the woman placed a coloring in book and crayons down in front of her.

"Cute bow, little one," she said before leaving the table to allow Dan and Nadia time to decide.

"Favorite place. This is it. This is my favorite place. I'm never leaving," Nadia said as she held up the packet of crayons for Dan to open.

Chapter 10

Dan, inspired by the hearty steak sandwich he saw others eating ordered one as well and for Nadia, he had ordered the fish and chips delighting her as the fish came out in fish shapes.

"Daddy this day is amazing," she said as he broke a piece of his burger off and let her try it.

"It's too spicy," she said, reaching for her sippy cup which Dan had placed on the table.

"I love that we don't have to be discrete here," he said as she sipped feverously.
After lunch, Dan held Nadia's hand as they walked down the street, smiling at the other people they met and Nadia beaming when she was complimented on how stunning her was in her outfit.

"I'm so pretty, Daddy, everyone thinks so," she gloated, making him laugh and roll his eyes.

"If we go into the toy store, you can only get one thing, alright? And only for $100 or less," Dan said, adding a price limit, knowing that Nadia would try to find the most expensive toy in the whole store if she could only have one. Snickering, Nadia knew why she was given a limit and wrapping her arms around Dan's, and she looked up at him with the big eyes he had first been captivated by.

"Thank you, Daddy," Nadia said, kissing his arm as he opened the door for her before they walked inside. As Nadia walked in, bubbles fell from the ceiling as the sensor set a bubble machine off delighting her and making her laugh as Dan waved them out of his way.

"Daddy, you're not meant to pop them!" Nadia happily giggled as she walked back over to Dan and took his hand, laughing as a bubble landed on her nose.

"Let's go over there," Dan suggested seeing the giant stuffies in the third row. Nadia was overcome with wonder as she looked up and down the shelves. Teddy bears, puppies, bunnies and kittens greeted her as she looked through the colors. Dan smiled and looked around, hoping there would be a chair, smirking when he saw another man sitting on a long lounge.

"Hey," Dan said, sitting down, giving the man a bro nod.

"Hi man. Get comfy, you'll be here a while if your little one is anything like mine," the man laughed.

"I'm Jeff," the man said, extending his hand.

"Dan," he replied, shaking Jeff's hand.

"First time?" Jeff asked, watching as Dan looked around at the customers in the store. He saw littles holding their caregiver's hands dressed in their little clothes and sucking on pacifiers. He saw a middle who was giving her Mommy attitude because she didn't want to leave the store without a spy toy she was clutching onto and he saw a little boy holding his Daddy's hand outside the store while his Daddy spoke on the phone.

"Is it that obvious?" Dan laughed as Nadia

came back with a large blue puppy stuffie.

"Daddy, may I please have this one?" Nadai asked, sitting on Dan's lap.

"Of course. Do you want to buy him yourself?" Dan asked, passing Nadia a $50 note. Nodding her head, she took the note and walked off to the counter.

"Sweet girl you've got there," Jeff said.

"Yeah, she's a keeper," Dan said, standing up and going to stand behind Nadia who was now being served by the cashier. Placing the puppy into Nadia's waiting arms, the cashier smiled at her as they left the store.

"I think I will name her, Starfish," Nadia giggled. Dan loved it when she was in one of her happy, silly moods and rolled his eyes at her dramatically.

"Starfish?" He questioned, only making Nadia continue to giggle.

"Yep. That's her name Daddy, Starfish," Nadia said, deciding that her joke was in fact now the toys serious name. Dan just laughed as he led her back to where the truck was parked.

"Time to go baby girl. I bet you are tired after such a big day," Dan said, ignoring Nadia who shook her head no as he buckled her into the front seat and placed her paci in her mouth, pulling her seat back until she was almost laying down.

"Shut your eyes little one, I know you're sleepy," Dan said, placing his hand on her tummy and patting her gently as he drove out of the street, back down the long road and out onto the street of the 'real world.' It felt as though he had been in a dream as he drove back to their apartment. The people in their adult clothes, the busy lives they seemed to be living. He had almost forgotten the feeling of stress, and as he saw people angrily talking into their phones. He looked over at Nadia, her eyes closed and her lips slightly pushed out around the pacifier in her mouth and sighed.

I don't know how life gets any better than this, he thought to himself.

"Daddy, do you think we should get a puppy?" Nadia said three weeks later. Since going to 'little world' which is what Nadia had taken to affectionately calling it, Nadia had become obsessed with puppies.

"A puppy?!" Dan said, almost choking on the cereal he was eating. Nadia just looked at him plainly as she nodded her head, fully expecting that her request would be granted. That had been the pattern she had come to know as true. All she had to do was continue to please Dan, following his rules, completing the tasks he had set for her, and she would be rewarded with whatever her heart desired.

"I don't know sweetie," he said, making her mind confused.

"What do you mean, Daddy?" She asked, trying not to sound disappointed. Dan put the newspaper he was reading down and looked at her. Her innocent face looking ever so slightly annoyed.

"Well, a puppy doesn't stay a puppy. It

turns into a dog, and dogs live for a very long time. What happens if you decide you want to up and go somewhere? What happens to the dog if we can't find a place which lets us move in with a dog?" Dan asked, folding the newspaper and looking directly at Nadia who had a serious look on her face.

"These are all good points, but, Daddy, I think you are missing something," Nadia said, putting her crayons down to match the attention Dan was putting on the topic.

"Which is?" He asked, slightly amused. This is what Dan loved about having Nadia as his little. She was polite and obedient, and she knew how to word her arguments in a way that wasn't bratty or irritating.

"We would move into a pet-friendly place first and then get the dog. We would only go on adventures which we could take the dog on, and anyway, you said you love camping, and you can always take a puppy on camping trips," Nadia explained, happy that Dan hadn't shut her idea down completely.

"I'll think about it," he said. Dan's answer translated in Nadia's mind as 'I need more convincing,' so she immediately got busy on her puppy marketing strategies as she found a blank piece of paper and began drawing puppies.

"What Daddy? It's the law of attraction," Nadia giggled, the mischief in her eyes entertaining Dan as he watched her, her cheeky grin unable to hide her delight in playing in the grey zone of their dynamic.

"We could take her to 'little world,'" Nadia casually said as she colored, Dan sipping his coffee and looking at her over the edge of his cup.

"Ok, what would you call her then?" Dan said, entertaining the idea. Nadia thought for a moment before taking out a blank piece of paper and scribbling down what looked like a list of names. Dan peered over the table to get a closer look and read the names Nadia was considering out loud.

"Evie, Scarlet, Harriet," Dan read, pausing at the last name.

"Harriet? Have you ever heard of a dog called Harriet?!" He said as his laughter escaped and caused Nadia to look at him with those playful eyes, he adored so much.

"Daddy!" She exclaimed, surprised that he would make fun of her choices.

"Ok, what else have you got. We are not having a dog called, Harriet," Dan laughed, rolling his eyes.

"Suddenly that's my favorite name," Nadia said looking at him with a slight challenge in her smirk.

"Like it all you want, it's not happening," Dan said, making his intention clear.

"What about Cupcake?" Nadia said, laughing as she tilted her head back.

"Alright, alright. Evie. What about Evie?" She suddenly said, realizing that Dan was not the least bit amused.

"Evie will do fine," he said, getting up to kiss her forehead.

"But I never said we are getting a dog, just

that I wanted to know what name you'd give it," Dan said, putting the dishes of their breakfast in the dishwasher.

"Mm-hmm," Nadia replied, knowing in her heart that it was only a matter of time before they got a dog.

"Hi, we'd like to look at the dogs. I don't really know how to say that any better, first time," Nadia said in her usual tactless manner making Dan smirk behind her. It had taken him less than a week to take her to the pound. She put it down to her silent protesting of puppy pictures and only wanting to hear stories about dogs as she fell asleep at night. Dan knew that they were only there because he couldn't see why he'd make her wait for a dog when it would hardly cause a dint in their lives, but he let Nadia think it was all her.

"Ok, head out back, and if you see one you like, you'll need to come back and fill out the paperwork and pay the fee," the lady at the counter said as she opened the back door which led to the barking dogs in kennels that made Nadia cringe.

"I'm not a fan," Nadia whispered to Dan as she looked around the sad faces of the dogs that starred back at her.

"Yeah, rough," Dan replied, bending down to look at a massive pitbull, the dogs eyes cautious of him. Dan stood back up and looked at Nadia, taking her hand in his.

"Maybe we've made a mistake," he said frowning.

"No. We haven't. We might just need to rethink," Nadia said which instantly made Dan nervous. Whenever Nadia had a thought that made her eyes glitter the way they did right now, he knew that they were in for an adventure.

"There's only four dogs in here. Let's get them all," Nadia said, Dan, closing his eyes and taking a breath.

"How are we suppose to choose just one?!" Nadia said, her heartbreaking as she saw the sad faces of the dogs. Dan opened his eyes and looked down at her, biting his bottom lip.

"Baby," Dan started to say, still deep in thought. Nadia just looked back at eyes that he knew he could hardly say no too.

"Look, little one. We simply don't have the space to put them. We can't look after four dogs," he said gently but seeing the unwavering reserve on Nadia's face.

"We can just buy a small house on a big bit of land out west," Nadia replied. This was another thing Dan loved about her. She had that, childlike hope that everything can be fixed. She didn't live in a world with constraints. She lived in a world where anything and everything was possible. He smiled, asking himself why he was acting like such an adult when his own spirit wanted to be as free as hers and just laughed as he nodded. His eyes looking into hers, her innocence beaming from them and her hero being him.

"I guess I better get that apartment of ours on the market for sale and not tenants hey, little one?" He said, smiling as she skipped next to him as they went back out to the front counter and buy all four dogs.

Chapter 11

"This is the coolest thing I've ever done!" Nadia said on the drive home. In the back seat of Dan's truck sat the massive Pitbull he had seen first which Nadia had called Evie, two Staffordshire Bull Terriers call Henry and Sasha, and a white Bull Arab Dan named Venus. Nadia watched how they rested against each other, accepting pats from her as she reached behind into the back seat.

"Baby, turn back around," Dan said as they drove through the city. They were on their way to the pet store, Dan explaining that he would go in and buy the basics but that they could go together to the store again once their new family was set up to buy special things for each of their new fur babies. Nadia had giggled happily, placing her feet on the edge of the seat and holding her knees together.

"I'll go to the real estate tomorrow to sort out the house situation. I want you to look for houses with a large patch of land, somewhere in the country I think, little one," Dan explained as he pulled into the pet parking lot and kept the air con running.

"Lock the doors when I get out sweetie," he said, kissing her on the forehead and patting the dogs before leaving the truck. Nadia took out her phone and quickly got to work, searching for property all over the state, hoping to find something suitable. It hadn't escaped her that they were living a life, not many of their friends or family understood. They would understand it even less once they learned of the new additions to the family and their potential new home. Nadia wondered when she had become so fearless, so free and so willing to explore all the possibilities the world presented. She flicked through the search, marking several properties that fit their budget and noted that they would really be making the country switch.

"How did you go?" Dan suddenly said opening the door after having put four dog begs, four collars and leashes, dog bowls, toys and two huge bags of dry food in the tray of the truck.

"So good. Oh my gosh, I hope you like them. I think this could be really fun," Nadia said, watching as Dan looked intently at a farm ranch two hours away.

"This one. Let's put an offer on it today. I can just see you plucking the flowers around this big old tree here in the middle of the yard and putting them in your hair, the pups running around happily. Baby, thank you for making my life so fun, it's sure as hell never boring with you," Dan said, handing her back the phone and driving out onto the road. He turned the radio up, rolled the windows down, and laughed how the dogs stuck their heads out of the windows wanting to feel as free as he and Nadia craved.

"This is living," he whispered, looking over at Nadia who let the wind sweep her hair, watching the people walk out of their office buildings, seeing their drained faces, wondering how he could have ever thought that that life was worth living.

They arrived home and took the dogs inside, setting up their beds in the living room and food bowls on the balcony outside.

"I'm pretty sure that we can't have animals in this building, even though you own it, Daddy," Nadia said, playing with the rope he had bought for the dogs.

"Shh, I won't tell if you don't," Dan said in a hushed tone, the look in his eye telling her everything she needed to know.

"I think you've been a big girl for about as long as I think you can stand. Come to Daddy little one, let me look after you," Dan said, not having to repeat himself as Nadia jumped into his arms and snuggled into his neck.

"Oh, I hadn't realized you were so close to being my sweet angel again. Did Daddy get you just in time?" Dan asked Nadia, putting her thumb in her mouth just to have Dan replace it with a pacifier. Nadia closed her eyes as he walked her to the bathroom, knowing that the dogs would be happy playing in the living room for a moment. He placed her down on the ground and closed the door behind them, taking of her adult clothes and putting them in the wash basket, turning the bath on and letting the tub fill with sweet-smelling bubbles before picking her up and lowering her into the warm water.

"Duckie?" Dan asked, seeing Nadia close her eyes and curl up into the fetal position.

"No thanks, Daddy," she replied, breathing deeply. She wasn't sure why she felt like this after being out of the house for hours at a time. It was almost as though she was a sponge and had absorbed too much water, not being able to take anymore, and shutting down was her only coping strategy that made sense. She felt her heart pounding as though she was having a panic attack, her head spinning with images and flashing lights she couldn't slow down.

"It's alright sweetie, just breathe, I've got you," Dan softly said, seeing her try to unwind in front of him.

"It hurts, Daddy," Nadia said softly.

"I know darling, just breathe. You're alright, you're safe, nothing bad is going to happen to you," he said, stroking her hair and gently washing her toned body. He had seen her go through this before and was glad that he finally knew how to help her. He turned the lights off, opened the shutters on the windows, and let the moonlight stream into the room — the neon lights reflecting on the ceiling. Nadia sighed, opened her eyes and breathed as though she had just ran up a hill as she tried to calm herself.

"Thanks, Dada," she said, whatever this feeling was, wash over her, and her heart returning to beating regularly.

"That was quick this time. I'm proud of you. I still think that it is post-traumatic stress baby," Dan said, taking a towel from the rail and help Nadia out of the bathtub.

"I don't know. I have another therapy session this week. I'll probs go and have to guess what is troubling me again," Nadia replied, discontent in her voice which just made Dan laugh.

"Then go to another therapist?" He suggested making Nadia shake her head.

"No I like her, she just makes me have to do the work and I'd much rather she just tell me what's wrong with me," she explained. Dan finished drying her off and took her hand as he opened the door to find the four dogs laying contently in the hallway, getting up as they saw the door open.

"Hi guys," Dan said, happy with their decision to buy all four dogs.

"So she helps stand you up but makes you take the steps on your own two little feet," he teased making Nadia laugh.

"I guess so," she yawned, stretching her body and arching it until she felt like it would snap before relaxing on the bed and watching as the dogs found a new spot on the floor. Dan went to the cupboard and took out a diaper, long-sleeved purple onesie, and black thigh high socks.

"Stay still for Daddy," Dan said, adding double thickness to the diaper before quickly fastening it around her waist.

"Daddy, I don't like it," Nadia said, squirming on the bed, feeling too big to be diapered so heavily.

"That's ok," Dan said, holding Nadia's ankles down and forcing her socks on.

"Don't be naughty for Daddy or you'll feel my hand on your pretty little ass," Dan growled making Nadia tense her calves. He had never had to punish her before, and she really wasn't interested in it happening tonight. She lay still and let Dan pull the onesie tight over her diaper and push the material into her pussy. Rubbing over her body, Dan smiled in satisfaction, patting her predatorily.

"There's my good girl," he said, reaching for her and lifting her effortlessly into his arms, carrying her back out into the living room and placing her down on the couch. Going into the kitchen, he took out steak and vegetables, beginning to cook as Nadia watched cartoons and played with the dogs.

Chapter 12

The apartment sold faster than Dan or Nadia had expected, and within a month they were needing to move out and into a new place. Having had no luck with buying a property, they decided to widen their search and had found an old farmhouse on a large property in a town that neither of them had ever heard the name before.

"What if it sucks?" Nadia said, driving through the town and looking back to check on the dogs. They looked back at her, their happy faces making her whole being feel alive. Dan had had custom made dog cages built, with the air-con system integrated so they would always be comfortable, depending on the weather. Nadia loved that Dan was so thoughtful like that.

"Well, I guess we won't get it," he laughed back, wondering why she would think they'd buy something which didn't suit them.

"Yeah I know, but we are running out of time, and I just think that maybe, we might need to like, renovate it something and that might be a good thing to keep in the back of our minds," Nadia explained. Dan looked at her, a sideward smirk spreading across his lips. He winked at her, reaching over to hold her hand, bringing it up to kiss it and squeezing it gently but excitedly.

"Ok. Don't worry, darling. I won't let us be homeless," Dan said, reading her mind even when she didn't want him to. Nadia just rested her head against the headrest and looked at him, tracing her fingers over his defined jawline, making him smile as he drove up the dirt driveway.

"I think we are here, little one," Dan said, peering out through the windscreen. Nadia raised an eyebrow.

"Time to play the big girl game," she laughed, making Dan smirk as they both got out of the truck, Dan greeting the agent who was waiting for them.

"The property is ready to go, all you'd have

to do move your furniture in, it really is such a steal especially in this current market," the real estate man. Dan knew that he knew him from somewhere and missed all the things he was telling them as he racked his brain, trying to figure out where he had seen him before. The man took them through the farmhouse, Nadia falling in love with it instantly. The bones of the house were solid, and she could picture how the new kitchen and bathroom would look, how the rooms would be made fresh with a bit of paint, but when she looked over at Dan, his mind was clearly elsewhere.

"What do you think?" The real estate man asked both of them. Nadia looked at Dan, who was still trying to figure out where he knew this man from.

"I think I'd like to take a look around the yard with the dogs," Nadia said, wanting to get Dan away and to herself to ask him what the hell he was doing. The man nodded, going into the spare room as he waited for Nadia and Dan to be finished with their inspection.

"What are you doing?" Nadia asked Dan as they opened the dogs' cages.

"I think I know him from somewhere," Dan said, taking Sasha down and letting her run after the other three as Nadia turned to look at him with disbelief.

"What?" He asked, curious as to why she had a problem.

"Daddy, have you even seen the house?" She asked, sighing and leaning against the truck.

"Yeah. I like it. What about you? Shall we put an offer on it?" He said, Nadia, rolling her eyes but nodding her head.

"That's it!" Dan suddenly said, Nadia, not amused one bit.

"He was the guy I met the first time we went to 'little world!' We were in the toy store. I sat down next to him," Dan said, feeling highly accomplished.

"That's great, Daddy," Nadia said, unsure about what this had to do with anything.

"I think we should put an offer in right now. Let's go do that," Dan said, whistling to the dogs who began to run back to them.

Dan and Nadia drove home after getting their offer accepted and signing papers, the nights' sky covering the windscreen.

"Daddy, I think your tummy is telling me that it wants to get take out," Nadia said, trying to sound as serious as she could but letting a small giggle escape.

"I think it's more your tummy than mine," Dan teased back checking the time.

"It is late, yeah fuck it, good call," Dan said, pulling into the first burger joint he found.

"Lol, yeah fuck it," Nadia replied, making Dan whip his head around at her in surprise.

"You know better than to swear like that little lady. I guess Daddy should have led by better example," Dan said, taking her out of the truck before putting the dogs on their leashes and tieing them to a post out the front.

"You want to stay with them for a minute. I know what you'll want. Double cheeseburger with a small fries and a large choc shake, extra sauce, no pickles," Dan said, making Nadia smile and tilt her head from side to side.

"Yep," she laughed.

Dan came back five minutes later, a tray in his hands and set it down on the table.

"Life is nice with you," he whispered in her ear and kissed her cheek, surprised when she turned her head and kissed him full on the lips.

"Woah," Dan said, pulling away, breaking the kiss and looking at Nadia with wide eyes.

"I want to, Dan," Nadia said, making Dan almost jump out of his seat with excitement. She had told him months ago that if he wanted to be with her, he'd have to wait a long, long time before he had her body in any kind of adult way. For the first time, she felt strong. She felt like sex wouldn't be something to force, something to fight. She wanted to know what it felt like to smile instead of frowning as she connected instead of being taken.

"I don't want you to think that just because we have this house now that you owe me or something," Dan said, making Nadia laugh.

"Don't flatter yourself," she said, rolling her eyes as her guard went back up. Taking a few mouthfuls of her burger before speaking again, he watched her with a curiosity that was never quenched.

"It's not like that. I am just ready, that's all," she softly said, the world fading all around them.

"So finish your fries. Coz I wanna ride your dick," Nadia whispered getting up and going to put her rubbish in the bin.

"Does this feel weird for you?" Dan said, unbuttoning his shirt in the moon light-filled room an hour later. Nadia just laughed and nodded her head.

"Like I've seen you naked heaps of times, you've seen me too, but this feels different," Dan said, kicking his shoes off.

"Different naked," Nadia agreed,

swallowing hard.

"What are you into?" Dan suddenly asked, realizing that he had never asked her how she liked to fuck before. Nadia froze for a moment, unsure how to answer that question.

"I don't know. I honestly don't. I've done a heap of stuff, sure, but was I into it. I'm not sure," she replied, standing in front of Dan with just her panties on.

"Ok, wanna try, like, everything then?" Dan said as if they had nothing to lose. Nadia just nodded and shrugged as she looked around the room nervously.

"This is dumb, why are we so nervous," she said, wanting to feel anything except for the feeling of vulnerability.

"I'm not nervous; you are," Dan laughed, surprised that his palms were getting sweaty.

Gross, he thought, going over to the bed and wiping them on a pillow before throwing it on the floor.

"Do you want to do this in bed?" Nadia

asked, seeing him sitting there, a dumb smile on his face.

"I guess, most people do at some point," he said, sighing and wishing he could shake the first time terrors he hadn't felt since high school.

"You got me feeling like a kid," Dan said, shaking his head.

"Welcome to my world," Nadia replied, making him laugh as she climbed into bed beside him.

"So. This is the story we are going to be telling? That we were both too scared actually to do anything, so we just made jokes all night?" Nadia said, laughing and looking down into her lap.

"I must say, it is really nice that we can make jokes thought," Dan said, Nadia, cutting him off by pressing her lips to his.

"Oh wow, we are really doing this," he muttered through the kiss.

"Yeah, we are," Nadia said, taking his hand and placing it on her body, smiling into the kiss as she felt him take over. He pulled her into his body, laying side by side as his fingers ran through her hair and over her breasts, feeling his dick surge with enjoyment as he squeezed them.

"You're wet," Dan said, sounding surprised.

"That's usually taken as a good sign," Nadia said as she rolled him onto his back and placed her hand on his chest as she reached behind and jerked his dick making him involuntarily gasp. Nadia moved down and felt his hard cock against her slit, pausing for a moment. She looked at him, with his loving eyes that seemed to read into her soul. His mouth that had never uttered anything but kindness and admiration. His hands which had only ever held her in the highest regard, as she slowly allowed him to enter her with gentle ease. Biting her bottom lip and closing her eyes as she lifted off him just to grind down again, she smiled.

"You've got me," Dan softly said as he sat up and held her to his lap, bucking his hips forward, Nadia wrapping her arms around his neck. She rested her head on his shoulder, placing her hand over his heart, feeling his pulse as he continued to fill her. Panting, he lay back down, turning over with Nadia's instigation and kissed her forehead feeling his senses heighten with each thrust. Holding himself up over her, she felt his muscled arms pulsate and his back rippled with intention.

"Dan," Nadia whispered, lifting onto her elbows as she kissed him, exploring him with more eagerness. He rested on his forearm and ran his fingers through her hair, down her cheek and wrapped his hand behind her head, holding her to him.

"I'm right where I want to be," she said, taking both hands and holding his face still, looking into his eyes, he buckled and dropped his body onto hers making her laugh and groan at the sudden weight crushing her body.

"Way to kill the mood," he said, on shaky arms trying to reposition himself, stopping when Nadia shook her head no.

"It's ok. Come here," Nadia said, pulling him back down on her smaller body. He rested his head against her neck, kissed along her collar bone and wrapped his arms around her.

"Well, I guess this is goodbye to my heart, it's yours now," Nadia said as she felt her orgasm begin to edge dangerously close.

"We can stop if you'd like," Dan said, never actually wanting to leave with bed with her. Nadia just shook her head as she took his hand and placed it on her ass, showing him how she wanted to be touched. Surprised, Dan slapped and groped at her fighting off his climax, desperate to cum with her instead.

"Oh, Nadia, god damn," he said, feeling her break, joining her immediately. She giggled as she felt him fill her, surprised that her usual reaction to want to go and have a shower, seemed to be non-existent with him. She lay there, in the bed with him, wrapped up in his arms and couldn't remember frowning once.

"That was different," she said, moving away from him and going to put a shirt on. Dan watched as she disappeared into the bathroom, only to see her come back a minute later. She was wearing the crimson lace panties he had seen her buy online but had never seen her wear and smiled at how her messy hair, white t-shirt, and sexy panties made him weak for her all over again.

"You really are the most beautiful woman I have ever seen, Nadia," Dan breathlessly said, feeling his heart beat for her in a way that it hadn't before tonight. She playfully posed for him, jumping back into bed and into his arms.

"Is this our life now? We have magical sex, live in the country with our big dogs? Don't have enter the rat race? I mean, I love it, but what are we going to do when the money runs out?" Nadia said, knowing that their work free bliss would not be able to be maintained forever. Dan deeply exhaled while he thought.

"Yeah, pretty much. I love magical sex with you, I've never felt so, I don't even know, powerful maybe? It's something more than strong, it's like I could be an air bender or something," Dan said, the bewilderment in his experience making Nadia smile to herself.

"Air bender? Ok, Mr Air bender. I think it might be like, alignment. Everything has gone from absolute chaos to peace, power, certainty, and balance," Nadia said, getting tickled as she teased Dan.

"I think that when we move into the town, we should look for jobs we can do online so that we can work to our own schedules. There are more jobs online than there is in the 'real world' so it might be a good move," Dan said, Nadia accepting immediately.

"Sounds good to me," she said, getting back up and holding her hand out to him.

"It's been fun, but I'm tired Daddy," Nadia said, instigating the return of their DDLG dynamic. Dan beamed and jumped into action, turning on the light and near blinding both of them.

"Daddy!" Nadia exclaimed as she covered her eyes but feeling Dan take her hand.

"Here I am," he said leading her to the bathroom and running a shower for the both of them. Soaping her body with the strawberry body wash she loved so much, she made bubbles with it, happy when Dan didn't pop them. Getting out, Dan knew how tired Nadia was by how quiet she had become and smiled lovingly at her. He dipped his head to see her eyes were closed while he dried her.

"Not much longer, baby girl," he said picking her up and taking her back to the bedroom. Ripping the sheets off the bed and quickly putting on new ones, before Dan lay Nadia down, he placed her matte black pacifier in her mouth and watched as she fell asleep almost instantly. Laughing to himself, he secured a diaper to her and gently dressed her in her favorite crimson long-sleeved onesie, making sure to push up the sleeves and tucked her up in bed. Dressing himself in long grey sweatpants, he joined her and cradled her in his arm, pressing her against his body as he organized how they move all their belongings to the new house while she slept.

Chapter 13

"Nadia, are you ever going to tell me what is it that keeps you up at night?" Dan said, suddenly over dinner three months later. They had successfully made the old farmhouse into a home they could both enjoy by repainting it and putting in a new kitchen and bathroom. The dogs were playing in the yard, and Nadia watched as they chased each other over logs and through the trees.

"I know that he just up and left one day, but there's more. I can see it little one, and I want to help you with it," Dan said, reaching out to hold her hand making her flinch and look at him before biting her bottom lip.

"Why do you even care. Most guys don't want to hear about the ex that still manages to ruin a perfect day," Nadia said, making Dan smirk.

"I'm not like most guys," he replied without missing a beat.

He has a point., she thought, shrugging her shoulders.

"Alright, here is it," she said, taking a deep breath and exhaling before looking at him.

"He called out, *it's dinner time,* as he washed his hands before coming back over to me. I was failing at trying not to be pouty," Nadia began to explain.

"He said, *I warned you what would happen if you weren't good for me, and now you're sulking?* I just looked at him angrily and shaking my head no," Nadia said, getting up and moving to sit on Dan's lap.

"*No? You're not bratty? Because this is not what not being bratty looks like,* he whispered to me before I told him I didn't need such a thick diaper. I pulled my puppy dog eyes, the ones which had served me so well in the past, but it didn't work. I was shocked when I saw him flex his hips forward and unbuckle his belt. Doubling it over, I swallowed hard, my eyes going wide and tensing my calves," she continued, feeling Dan's arms wrap around her waist.

"*Get over my lap;* he had calmly said, which just made me more nervous. I slowly obeyed, hoping that he wasn't going to go hard on me. Rubbing my ass, he placed his other hand on my throat and gently caressed my skin, feeling for my pulse, smiling as he felt it race." Nadia reached for her sippy cup, not wanting to remember what came next, the memory which still haunted her even on perfect days.

"*Breath*, he whispered almost lovingly, only adding to my confusion. He took his time running the belt over the exposed flesh of my thighs and laughed when body involuntarily shivered, goosebumps covering my skin," she said before biting her bottom lip, looking at Dan's gentle eyes for reassurance.

"*Daddy, please don't,* I softly begged, a tear escaped and fell onto the couch. *But how will you learn not to complain to me about your diaper if I don't sweetie?* He teased, continuing to trace my body with the belt. Looping it around my neck and pulling it until he heard me choke. Wrapping the strap around his fist, he pulled, jerking my head back, forcing a breathless gasp to escape as my eyes began to water. *Does being a bad girl for Daddy still feel like a good idea?* He had whispered in my ear as his hand came down hard on my left thigh, making me bite my bottom lip and close my eyes." Nadia stood up and paced the room, unsure of how she had ever let herself be used so viciously.

"*No, Daddy*, I replied as another spank landed on my right thigh. I felt the sting burn on the softest parts of my body as he continued to spank me, making my legs go red, the skin rising. I knew that they were being to welt. I lost count and stopped wincing against the impact and simply allowed him to have me. My body fell limp on his lap. My head dipped as the leather belt crushed into my wipe pipe. Feeling my surrender, finally stopped and supported held my head as he loosened the belt and took it from my neck. Placing it down next to him and turning me over, I guess he was surprised at how glassy eyes my eyes were. I just blankly stared at the ceiling." Nadia explained, sitting against the wall and getting covered by dog cuddles.

"*Baby?* He asked, clicking his fingers in front of my face, waiting for my eyes to focus on him, smiling at me when they slowly did. *Are you alright, darling? I'm sorry I had to do that, Daddy doesn't like having to punish you, but I will not let you be a brat,* he said, as my gaze looked back at him with emptiness. *Come on, let me remind you that you are the most special part of my life,* he said, picking me up and taking me into the bedroom, pulling the sheets down and lowering my limp body into bed. But I was done, there was nothing he could do to make up how far he had gone, nothing I could do to take back how silent I had fallen," she said, Dan getting up to make a cup of sweet tea. He hated stories like this, the ones where the people who are meant to look after someone simply, don't.

"*Can you talk to me?* He asked, getting

slightly annoyed that I seemed to have lost my light, my sparkle. I just looked back at him, unsure of what I was meant to say. Closing my eyes, I turned around and away from him, only making him more annoyed. Reaching for my shoulder, he turned me back around, glaring into my face, but my eyes staring straight through him. *Nadia, don't be like this, you know that if you broke a rule, that this would be the punishment,* he said, only to be again greeted with my back once more as I turned over and let my tears silently fall onto the pillow as he sighed angrily and walked out of the room, shutting the door behind him," Nadia explained, wiping a tear that fell on her cheek as she got up and walked into the kitchen. Sitting up on the bench, she swung her legs on the bench as she sipped the tea Dan had made for both of them.

"I thought for days about it. I'd leave for work really early and get home way after the city had closed. I just kept thinking, Why didn't I just stop him? He never actually wanted to hurt me. He would have stopped. He would have fucking stopped. But I just didn't think about it at the time. I was so obsessed with doing what I was told, hoping that I'd be given the smallest of kindnesses after," Nadia continued, shrugging her shoulders as Dan stood in front of her and placed his hands on her thighs.

"Did you ever have a conversation with him about what had gone down?" Dan asked. Nadia loved that this was his first reaction to communicate. She had been surprised at how solution based he was when they had first gotten together, but now it just made her heart dance, that in the midst of his anger, he would always stop and redirect the discussion towards a solution.

"Kinda, I told him, *it was really not cool what I let you do. I'm not down for that kind of impact, you gave me fucking nothing afterward, and I really don't trust you anymore. I'm coming home to talk about this with you. I should have said red. I take full responsibility for that. But I also think you shouldn't have been such a dickhead when you didn't get your way.* He tried to be playful, but I just shook my head and said, *Don't. There's like zero dynamic here right now. I'm trying to fix this. I'm trying to stay when all I want to do is run away and smash in all the windows on your truck.* He didn't think that was as endearing as I had tried to make it sound," Nadia explained making Dan laugh. He picked her up and took her to the couch, sitting her in her blanket nest and cuddling her as she continued to share her story.

"He goes, *I know I fucked up. I shouldn't have gone so hard on you. You did break a rule though,* and I said, *I broke a rule yes, I didn't deserve to be pushed that far. I can accept that I didn't look after myself, but I thought I could trust you and if you can't even take responsibility for your part then, what the fuck are we even doing here?* He couldn't answer me so I just rolled my eyes and said, *well, that's that then,* and I just turned and walked away out of the apartment, as I decided he could keep my clothes," Nadia said to a speechless Dan.

Dan sat at the table in silence, surprised that Nadia

had been so badly treated by someone who was meant to be the one person in the world that wouldn't hurt her. Silently grateful that it hadn't worked out with anyone else so that he could have her all to himself.

"I'm so sorry that happened to you. How sick and twisted, as if he couldn't see he had pushed you past your limit, no one is that stupid," Dan said, leaning over and kissing her forehead.

"It doesn't matter," Nadia began to say, getting cut off by Dan who placed his finger to her lips.

"Don't say that. It does matter, or you wouldn't still be broken by it," he corrected, making her resent that he was right but love that he knew her well enough to be able to call her out on it.

"Come on, you've told me, but you should write about it," Dan said, getting up and opening the back door, a gush of cold air flooding the house making Nadia's heart dance.

"See? The night is calling you, come on. I'll

get some candles and whiskey, and the dogs can play. Maybe I'll light a little fire, and we can roast marshmallows," he said, walking around the house collecting the things they would need for their impromptu evening under the stars.

Nadia stayed out as the night grew late, Dan coming out to light some candles and sip whiskey as she wrote on her laptop.

I did it. I survived it all. I knew I'd find happy one day and that one day finally happened. I got to the top, I finished the race, and now I'm looking around, and all I know is that now that I'm at the top, I won't let anything or anyone hurt that precious little one who still lives inside of me. Ain't no one going to take her hand and pull her down again. I used to think that strength was hard and cold and angry, but it isn't. It's something between peace and crying, somewhere in the middle of a heart that beats a pace to fast and eyes that let tears fall. It's a place next to hell and sorry, and I guess I'll do better next time. Kinda like when the sky breaks with blinding sunlight that's almost trying to burn your eyes out but helping you too clearly see after an overcast day. I don't know when I decided that I needed to become myself. Maybe it had just become too heavy carrying this sack of shit around. Maybe it was when I felt sick to my stomach every time I was hugged. It was probably when I couldn't breathe without feeling like it was still happening. I sure did give them more than I'd taken, I was too hard on myself, and I was broken and didn't know how to ask for help. I just allowed it to carve out some awful version of who I could be and in its wake, let go of everything good and true and real. Healing hasn't been what I thought it'd be. It's more like going ten rounds with the bruising only coming through in the morning. The real pain starts a few days later when you can hardly get your heavy heart out of bed, the weight of it needing to be carried with two hands when you are alone.

Too bad that you're going into battle for the next five days, too bad that you can hardly breathe your tears back, too bad that you can't bleed for them when you are so busy being your own champion. Nadia took her hands from the keyboard and read her words out loud; the melody almost lyrics from a sad country song. She looked at the tumbler of whiskey sitting next to her laptop, the wooden table making the yellow liquid look darker as she swirled it in the crystal glass. Bring it to her lips, she breathed in the scent and let it burn her mouth before swallowing more than she could hold, spilling it from the side of her mouth as she gasped as it stripped her throat. Looking at Dan, curled up on the chair in the corner, a blanket over him and surrounded by dogs, she knew he would be asleep till morning. She knew that she had tonight. It was rare that she was awake when he was not and yet, it was in the stillness of the late of night that she found herself sitting there in the dark back porch, her laptop keyboard light and the nearly burnt out candles eliminating the space.

I wonder if anyone can feel me sitting here, open, vulnerable, tipsy, and thinking about marrying him, she considered, putting her earphones in and finding the songs which soothed her wild, torn heart.

I just need to get my money right, give him the ring he deserves, give him the proposal that will take his breath away, and make him cry. I wish I could do it now, take him to the place, have the ring made, scream from the bottom of heart, the depths of my soul, will you marry me? Maybe my heart needed to be torn open so I could hold all the love I have for this man? Maybe it all went down like this so I wouldn't lose him, so I would know that when I found him, I could run but would never need too. I guess I had to learn to count on myself so I would know how much I needed to rely on him. That if he couldn't match me, then we'd never be a match. I guess I'm not hiding anymore, and that is as equally as scary as it is lovely. Nadia smirked as she rolled her eyes and yawned, finally tired as the clock inside struck 2 am.

"Baby girl, what are you doing? How are you still awake?" Dan asked in his sleepy voice, rubbing his eyes and blinking slowly.

"I'm just finishing off my journal entry, Daddy. I can't sleep tonight. I needed to get this out of my system. You may have been right about that," Nadia replied as he picked her up, sitting down where she had been and placing her on top of his lap, reading her laptop screen.

"Deep, bubba!" He exclaimed, kissing her shoulder and holding her close.

"Do you like it?" Nadia asked hoping that he wouldn't be mad about the stuff she wrote about marrying him. Nodding, Dan looked up at her and chuckled.

"I had just assumed that I'd be the one proposing, do you want to do it?" He asked her, playfully biting into her.

"I think so, I think I'd feel too trapped if you did it," Nadia replied, biting her bottom lip. Dan thought for a moment, before sticking out his bottom lip.

"I love that you always keep things so interesting. I'm excited to see what ring you'll get me! I don't have such a big ego that I can't let you do it. When and if you feel like it is right," Dan said, kissing Nadia on the cheek before standing up and carrying her into their bedroom, tucking her in and holding her as she fell asleep, a smile on her lips and peace in her heart as she spoke the words which always melted his heart.

"I love you, Daddy," the last words uttered for the day, the only ones he ever needed to hear.

Who is Tina Moore?

Tina Moore has enjoyed the lifestyle of a Mommy Domme for several years. She began exploring kink and BDSM in her youth and found her love of being a strict Mommy Domme in early 2000. Tina Moore is now an author of many MDLG, DDLG and ABDL themed novels.

Follow her on:

Author Page on Amazon

Instagram @tinamoore.kdp

If you enjoyed this book, it would be much appreciated if you leave **a review on Amazon**.